Worlds of Wonder

Emily Martha Sorensen

Also by Emily Martha Sorensen

Books:

Black Magic Academy

Comics:

A Magical Roommate
(available online)

To Prevent World Peace
(available in-print or online)

To my twins,
Simon and Nicodemus,

whose sleepless nights
gave me ample time to work on this,
instead of the book I was writing.

Table of Contents

Rite of Passage

Jaeda waved her arms in frustration. Yards of fabric billowed as her aunt attempted to pin back two enormous sleeves.

"I hate ceremonial robes," Jaeda muttered.

"Stop moving while I'm trying to fix this," Aunt Shaena murmured, her mouth full of pins. "Aha! Got it!" She stood back and beamed. "Don't you look *beautiful?*"

Jaeda frowned at the wavy reflection in her aunt's best mirror. "Beautiful" wasn't the first word she would use to describe herself, not when she was covered with sunburn and freckles. The ceremonial robes, which were way too big, didn't help either.

"These were your mother's robes, you know," Aunt Shaena said proudly, spinning Jaeda around to get a full view of her. "You look lovely. Just as she did before *her* Passage."

Jaeda avoided her aunt's eyes. Talk about her parents made her uncomfortable. It had been a year since their parents died in a boating accident, a year since she and Kaedin had come to live with Aunt Shaena, whom they'd never liked. And now here they were, their Rite of Passage next month, with no parents to dress them for it.

"Hey, Auntie, are you done yet?" A sunburned, freckled boy pushed his face through the tent opening. His eyes fell on his twin sister, and he chortled. "Boy, does that look bad on you . . ."

"*Out! Out!*" Aunt Shaena made shooing motions at him. "Your fitting's next!"

"Not today, it's not," Kaedin smirked. "Laeran and I are sailing. Coming, Jaeda?"

"You bet!" Jaeda yanked the ceremonial gown over her head and dumped it on the ground. Her aunt gasped in horror and snatched it up.

Jaeda brushed off the boy clothes she always wore, pulled on her sandals, and stuck her tongue out at her brother.

"Don't you dare leave!" Aunt Shaena cried. "We haven't finished our fitting yet!"

Jaeda turned back, trying to look innocent. "But, Aunt," she said, "where Kaedin goes, I go. Everyone knows that."

Aunt Shaena was still sputtering as she and Kaedin ran to the boat.

It was supposedly forbidden to go to the Isle before your Rite of Passage, but everyone did it anyway. The twins had gone particularly often in the past year, since they'd needed a place to escape from Aunt Shaena. Adults rarely came here.

"What do you think will happen when we go in?" Jaeda wondered aloud, running a finger along one of the carvings on the stone door. The carvings looked like writing, but no one could read it. "What talents do you think we'll get?"

"You'll probably become a dress-mage, like Aunt Shaena," Kaedin smirked.

Jaeda chucked a pebble at him. He ducked, laughing.

"Maybe you'll get magic," Laeran offered. "No one's gotten that in decades."

"I'd *love* magic!" Kaedin cried.

"Yeah, that would be practical," Jaeda snorted. "You're too lazy already."

"Hey, we're shoo-ins," Kaedin persisted. "The last people who got magic were twins, weren't they?"

"*Identical* twins," Jaeda shot back. "We're not."

Kaedin stared at her with wide eyes. "Since when?"

"Are you saying I look like a boy?" Jaeda asked indignantly.

"Maybe he thinks he looks like a *girl*," Laeran hissed.

"Hey!" Kaedin cried.

Jaeda rolled the pebble around in her fingers.

"I can't help worrying, though . . ." She swallowed. "I mean, no one ever remembers what happens there. And some people never come back. So suppose . . .?"

"We're not going to die," Kaedin scoffed. "We'll come back with magic."

"But they say it always takes the brightest and best — doesn't that worry you?"

"Why should it? It's not like we've lost anybody we know."

"It took my brother," Laeran said quietly. "Six years ago. Remember?"

Kaedin blinked.

"I, uh . . . I forgot about that," he said.

Laeran grinned slightly. "Well, I wouldn't worry. You two are hardly brightest or best."

Kaedin made a face at him.

"Let's go," Jaeda said, standing. "I ought to finish that fitting before Aunt Shaena complains to somebody."

Kaedin looked relieved. "Okay. Good idea."

Laeran nodded and got up, silently.

"It's *freezing*," Jaeda hissed to her brother, shivering in her oversized robes. Aunt Shaena had refused to resize them, insisting that would be a waste of fabric. "Do we really *have* to go this early in the morning?"

"We were born this early in the morning," Kaedin said gloomily, trudging towards the boat beside her. His robes made him look like a bulky sack.

"I think I hate tradition," Jaeda muttered.

"Welcome, Jaeda and Kaedin," the village leader intoned, holding out his hands as they neared the boat. *His* robes fit perfectly. "Your twelfth birthday has come. The day of your Rite of Passage has begun. I shall show you the way to the Isle."

"Doesn't he know we've been there dozens of times before?" Jaeda hissed.

"I think he assumes people will obey rules," Kaedin whispered back.

The village leader rowed them to the Isle mind-numbingly

slowly. Jaeda tried to grab the oars once, but the man smacked her hands away.

"Just trying to help," Jaeda muttered, slouching against her side of the boat.

They made it to the Isle, then to the stone door against the cliff.

"Place your hands on the sealed door," the village leader instructed. "It will recognize you as the proper age and permit you entrance."

Exchanging a glance, Jaeda and Kaedin pressed their hands on the door. They jumped back, startled, as the thick stone vanished.

"Magic," Kaedin breathed, looking excited.

"You must now enter," the village leader intoned. "I shall wait until the rise of the next sun. If you have not returned by then, a boat will be left in case of return later."

Both twins nodded. Jaeda's mouth felt dry.

The village leader stood there, staring at them meaningfully. It took several seconds for Jaeda to realize he was waiting for them. Kaedin reached out and grabbed her arm.

His hand was clammy. It was a relief to know he was scared, too.

Together, they stepped into the darkness.

At first there was nothing. Then came a blinding flash of light, and then —

White.

Everything — walls, ceilings, floors — white.

"It kind of glows, look," Kaedin whispered, tapping one of the walls. There was a hollow sound. "This is weird."

Jaeda glanced back at the entrance, and yelped to see it was gone. Everything was solid, smooth, white wall now.

"Welcome!"

She spun, her heart pounding, and scooted closer to her brother as a stranger strode towards them. There was a dark doorway on the other end of the room that had not been there a second ago.

"Wh-who are you?" Kaedin demanded.

The man stopped about ten feet from them.

"My name is Railan," he said. He looked them up and down. "Are you twins?"

Jaeda nodded nervously.

The man laughed. "Excellent! I haven't seen twins in years. What are your names?"

"Jaeda?" Jaeda said uncertainly.

"Kaedin," Kaedin declared.

"Good. You're not as frightened as some. That's a good sign. May I show you something?"

Jaeda and Kaedin glanced at each other. Nodded.

The man pulled some kind of stick from his pocket and tapped it on the wall beside him. Pictures dashed across it, too fast for Jaeda to catch even a glimpse of each.

"Magic!" Kaedin cried, looking excited.

The man laughed and tapped the wall again. The pictures vanished. "No, no, science. Well, they could be the same thing, I guess."

"Who are you?" Jaeda demanded, fighting to keep a quaver out of her voice. "What are you doing here?"

The man blinked. "Straight to the point, I see. All right." He cleared his throat. "I'm here because — ahem — Anthropological Experiment #649 requires authorization by all test subjects before beginning surveillance."

Jaeda blinked.

"What?" she and Kaedin asked.

The man coughed again. He looked uncomfortable. "The village you're from — along with others, spread out across your planet — was artificially created, centuries ago. We terraformed your world to be inhabitable and asked for volunteers to populate it. A few thousand came, agreed to have memories of their previous lives erased and replaced with new ones, and consented to have the rest of their life-memories recorded for our use after their deaths. This was in concordance with Ethics Law #276."

Jaeda stared at him, confused.

"Wait a minute," Kaedin said slowly. "You're saying . . . our world . . . our village . . . is fake?"

The man coughed. "Well, in a manner of speaking . . . yes."

"Why are you telling us this?" Jaeda demanded. "Do *you* get something out of it?"

"Straight to the point again, I see," the man said, looking amused. "And yes. According to Ethics Law #289, we can't continue the experiment unless we have each person's consent. So we bring you here at twelve years old, receive consent, and then implant a wafer to record your memories for the rest of your life. We naturally also erase any memories of time here, so we don't contaminate the experiment."

"The rest of our *life?*" Jaeda cried, appalled. "People are going to see our *thoughts?*"

"Not till you're dead," the man said hastily. "And in return, we give everyone a talent of their choice. It's a fair exchange."

"We get to *choose* our talents?" Kaedin cried, his eyes lighting up.

"I think we should discuss this first," Jaeda hissed.

"Magic!" Kaedin went on eagerly. "You can do that, right?"

"Magic?" the man repeated, looking doubtful.

"Yeah, moving things without touching them, and —"

"Oh, *that* . . ." The man looked uncomfortable. "Well, it's possible, but I wouldn't recommend it. The procedure's dangerous, and even with a volunteer, the number of deaths caused by —"

"Well, we don't care about risks." Kaedin rubbed his hands together. "We want magic."

"No, we *don't!*" Jaeda burst out.

Kaedin gaped at her.

"You *don't* want to be a dress-mage, do you?" he asked, horror in his voice.

"No, you idiot." Jaeda glared at him. "I don't give my *consent.* I don't want my memories recorded for experiments."

"Aw, come on," Kaedin pleaded. "It's fair. We could get magic!"

"No." Jaeda stared at the man, folding her arms. "It's not fair. I won't do it. Does that mean you have to kill me?"

Kaedin gaped beside her.

"No," Railan said slowly. "We don't do that. But without consent, we can't send you back."

"What then?" Jaeda demanded.

"Well, then . . ." The man swallowed. "Then you'd have to leave this world. Become a member of ours. And believe me, that would not be easy."

"Laeran's brother!" Kaedin gasped. "Is that what happened to him?"

The man nodded.

Jaeda focused on the walls. White. Stark white. So different, so strange. So alien.

She loved the village. She loved rowing, loved her brother, loved her friends' good-natured teasing. She wanted to learn to play the rock-flute. She wanted to be old enough to badger the adults to take her hunting.

Yes, their parents were gone, but she still had so much to lose.

Jaeda closed her eyes. The cost was high. But she still had to pay it.

"I'll do it," she said quietly. "I'll leave."

"*No!*" Kaedin cried. "Where I go, you go, remember?"

Jaeda ducked her head. She couldn't answer. Couldn't face him.

Silence reigned for a long moment.

"All right," Kaedin said, at last. "I'm going too."

Jaeda's head jerked up. She gaped at him.

"Where *you* go, *I* go." Kaedin lowered his voice. "Besides, I can always make them give me magic later."

The man had a curious smile on his face.

"Well, if you're sure . . ."

"We are," Jaeda and Kaedin chorused.

The smile widened. "Then you're in for the same path I chose. Please . . . follow me."

A Phone Conversation

"White House."

The little boy breathed heavily into the phone as he talked. "Hello, is this McDonald's?"

The president paused from emptying out old files from his desk. "This is the President of the United States speaking." He cleared his throat meaningfully. "On an unlisted number."

"Oh." The little boy exhaled loudly for a moment. "I guess I called the wrong place. I thought I was calling McDonald's."

The president clicked a button to record their conversation. He somehow doubted that. "Where did you get my unlisted phone number from?"

The voice sounded puzzled. "I dunno. I pressed the name on Mommy and Daddy's list."

"List?" The president sat up, suddenly alert. "List of what?"

"List of people I should call in case someone came in when they weren't home and I was, and my sister just came in, and they haven't come back with my Happy Meal yet."

There was a long pause. "I — see. A Happy Meal, you say."

"The kind with toys in it."

The president took a deep breath, trying to work out whether the child was sincere, or if this was a crank call. The latter seemed much more likely. "Happy Meals usually do. Do your parents leave you alone often?"

"Not when my sister's here."

The president leaned back in his chair, rubbing his eyes. He had more important things to do; the sooner he cleared this mystery up, the better. "No supervisor?"

"I don't need one."

"Little children shouldn't be left in the house alone."

The boy sounded puzzled. "If they didn't leave me, they couldn't go anywhere."

The president frowned at the phone. "They *could* take you with them, couldn't they?"

The boy panted loudly. "I'm not allowed out of the house until I metamorphose."

The president struggled to keep his temper in check. "Why don't you hang up and try not to dial my number next time?"

"Okay."

Click.

Ring, ring!

The president snatched at the phone on his desk. "Hello?"

The voice was familiar. "Oh, I guess it's you again."

Click.

Ring, ring!

"Hello?"

The child's voice sounded amazed. "Is it still you?"

The president clenched his teeth. "It's still me." He pressed the recording button again. Why on *Earth* weren't his calls being screened?

The little boy spoke in a confidential whisper. "I think Mommy and Daddy programmed the caller wrong, 'cause I keep pressing the McDonald's name, but I'm not getting McDonald's."

The president fought to control his temper. This crank call was no longer funny. "Where did your parents get this number from?"

There was silence for a moment, punctuated by heavy breathing. "Dunno. I guess from those files."

"What files?"

"The ones they find all the numbers from."

The president's mind raced. A child whose parents worked in the White House? Or perhaps were hackers? Of course, it was more likely that this *caller* was a hacker who thought crank calls were exceedingly funny.

They weren't.

The president tried to keep his voice level. "May I speak with your parents?"

"They're not home right now."

The president struggled to avoid sounding annoyed. "Right. You mentioned that. Where are they? Do they have a cellphone?"

"I dunno what a cellphone is."

"Tell me their names, and I'll have them paged."

"What's paged?"

"It means I call their names on a loudspeaker."

"What's loudspeaker?"

The president fought his temper under control again. "Just tell me their names and where they are!"

"They're Mommy and Daddy, and I dunno where they are."

The president ground his teeth. "Estimate."

"I dunno. Probably halfway between Alpha Centuri and Sol, if the lines weren't long." The little boy added, in his confidential whisper, "I don't like it when the lines are long. I get hungry, and then I go into hibernation and it takes *forever* to wake up, and when I do, my food's all cold."

This joke had gone far enough. The president jabbed a button to trace the call. It came up negative. "Where are *you?*"

"In my house."

The president ground his teeth. He'd forgotten how maddening little boys could be. He could deal with congressmen, but little boys were something else. "What's the address?"

"I dunno. It's too long."

"It's not good to forget your address. What would you do if you got lost?"

"I'm not allowed out of the house until I metamorphose."

The president's temper broke free. "This is no longer funny! I want to know where your parents are and how you found my *private, unlisted* number!"

The little boy breathed heavily into the phone. "I dunn—"

There was a high-pitched scream, and a series of thumps.

"Hey, sis, get your tentacles off the caller! That's *mine!*"

Then the line went dead.

The Spinning Talent

"Aria, you idiot!" Della shouted as her roommate walked in through the door, humming dreamily to herself. "What did you think you were doing down there?"

"I'm in love," Aria told her, falling happily onto her bed and staring up at the ceiling. "He promised he'd come back tomorrow, Delly! And I gave him Papa's old ring to remember me by —"

"That's what I meant," Della moaned, putting her head in her hands. "The headmistress will kill me when she finds out I let you give that away. It was enchanted to protect you from your birth-curse!"

"But who better to protect me than my true love?" Aria asked earnestly. "Besides, I don't believe I have a birth-curse. Papa's overprotective, that's all."

"This is supposed to be a school for the intelligent," Della groaned. "How did you even get in?"

"Daddy's rich," Aria shrugged, staring dreamily at the ceiling. "And I know I'm not as smart as you are, but nobody is, so there. Besides, he's my true love, and everyone knows true love conquers all!"

"Exactly *how* long have you known your 'true love'?" Della asked nastily.

"I've seen him from a distance before," Aria sighed happily. "But we've never spoken till now. Oh, Delly, wait till I tell you all about him! He's so handsome and brave and smart and witty, and he danced with me all night, and —"

"At the ball you went to *after* curfew," Della muttered.

"That's the one," Aria murmured. "And, oh, so *handsome!* I never realized from a distance just how *handsome* he is! Just wait till I tell you how we met —"

"I'm not interested in hearing how you met," Della snarled. "I don't even care who he is. Just make sure you get that ring back tomorrow, you hear?"

"Oh, Delly, you're so obsessed." Aria pouted. "His true love will protect me better than any old enchantment could. Just look at history."

"You're flunking history."

"Oh, don't bother me with lessons while I'm basking in true love's light!" Aria cried, flinging her arms out. "What do I need with school when I have *him?*"

Della groaned loudly, pinching out the candle by her bed. "Will you please promise to get your ring back from him the next time he drops by?"

"Oh, Delly!" Aria giggled uncontrollably. "You miss the point completely!"

To Della's fury, Aria spent the next three weeks sneaking out past curfew, chattering about her "true love" to every other girl who would listen, and evading every conversation about her ring. Her true love was apparently the second prince of the royal family, at least according to her horde of admiring classmates.

"Oh, he's so gorgeous," Lesias whispered, peeking just over the top of Della's dorm window to watch them. "Everyone says Havol's going to inherit the throne, but Tendar's the cutest. Aria's so lucky, I could just *die!*"

"Don't die," Della said sourly, "and get out of my room. Both of you."

"Oh, but I haven't had my turn yet!" Stellar cried, leaping up from Aria's bed. "Lessie, let me see! Please! Just one peek!"

"I don't suppose she's asked for her ring back yet?" Della muttered.

"OH, GOSH!" Lesias cried. "Stellar, look! They're *kissing!*"

That did it. Della slammed her textbook shut and stormed downstairs to the library. How could she expect to keep her scholarship if nobody would let her study?

Two weeks later, the headmistress called an all-school assembly about a truly horrifying prospect.

"King Jerold has announced a wish to find a new goldspinner," she informed the chattering crowd. "To facilitate this, we'll be holding tests for the spinning talent all day. Once you've been tested, you may have the rest of the day off, though normal classes will resume tomorrow."

Excited buzzing broke out among the crowds of girls.

"The spinning talent!" one of Aria's friends cried rapturously. "Imagine if I had it! Goldspinners don't have to worry about *anything* — they're in highest demand of *anyone!*"

"If I had the spinning talent, I wouldn't have to worry about marrying rich," another girl giggled, clapping her hands. "I could choose whatever cute husband I wanted, and make us *both* wealthy."

"I'd like to spin straw into gold," Stellar said dreamily. "Then Aria wouldn't be the only girl here with a chance at winning a prince."

Della listened in cold horror as the headmistress announced where the testing would take place and the order they'd be tested in. She didn't want to take a goldspinning test, didn't want to take the risk that she might pass it. Her grandfather had had that talent, and he'd been worked to an early grave as a result.

Besides, who wanted suitors who only liked you for your gold?

"It's fairly easy," the history mistress told Della, threading several long, thin straws through her wheel. "You spin this, chant the words, and see if anything happens. Are you enjoying that book about King Jerold's great-grandfather, by the way?"

"Oh . . . yes," Della said nervously. "Interesting man. He *really* used to be a beast before some princess kissed him?"

"Most historians suspect lycanthropy," the history mistress said. "Which means it may not have actually vanished. But it doesn't really matter as long as true love won, now does it?"

"Sure," Della muttered, her stomach tied in knots. She glanced across the room, where Aria was struggling to thread straws through the spokes of her wheel. The protocol mistress, looking exasperated, pulled the straws away from her and demonstrated how to use the wheel properly.

"Well, go on!" the history mistress smiled, patting Della on the shoulder. "Let's get this over with!"

Hands shaking, Della adjusted the spindle and twitched the straws into place. She'd used spinning wheels before, back home, but never for this — never to attempt this.

She squeezed her eyes shut and took hold of the wheel.

If I say the words wrong, there's no way it'll work.

"Straw into glunnnmmmb," she muttered. "Stlllmmmmm into gllllrrrd. Stlaaaa into . . ."

"ARIA!"

Della's eyes flew open. She jumped to her feet, knocking her wheel over.

Aria lay slumped across her own spinning wheel, its spindle clutched upside down in her hand. She didn't appear to be breathing.

Della ran to her fallen roommate.

"Aria!" she cried. "Aria! Wake up! Wake up, wake up, wake up, and *breathe,* you idiot!"

Aria gasped, and kept breathing. But her face remained still.

"I — I — I don't know what happened!" the geography mistress was babbling, near tears. "She just seized it, and it pricked her finger, and — and look what happened!"

A crowd of girls leapt up from their spinning wheels, clustering around Aria and murmuring excitedly.

"Out of the way!" a loud voice barked, pushing through them. Through a haze of tears, Della recognized the face of their headmistress.

"What happened here?" the headmistress demanded. "Was she starving herself? Does she need her corset loosened?"

A babble of excited theories sprang up from the crowd of girls around Aria.

"SHUSH!" the headmistress shouted, cutting them off. "Della, you're her roommate — do you know what caused this?"

"N-n-no," Della stammered, her whole body shaking. "I mean, she ate like a horse — she doesn't lace her corsets too tight — headmistress, I think it might have been her birth-curse!"

Gasps rang across the whole room.

"Didn't she have a ring to protect herself from that?" the headmistress demanded, her voice dangerous. "I recall her father saying she had to keep it on at all times."

"There's no ring on her fingers!" a girl called from the crowd.

Della gulped back a sob. "She — she gave it to a — a suitor, a few weeks ago."

"And you didn't inform me *immediately?*" the headmistress roared. "That neglect may have cost your roommate her life!"

Della burst into tears.

"*You!*" the headmistress shouted, pointing at the history mistress. "Find out who that boy was, and get it back!"

"I know who the boy was!" Lesias squeaked. "It's Tendar, our second prince! He's Aria's true love!"

"Prince?" The headmistress's voice sounded hoarse. "Prince of *our* kingdom? The king never answers inquiries. We'd never get through in time . . ."

Della shook all over.

My fault, she thought numbly. *This is my fault. If I had just told the headmistress, instead of worrying I'd get her into trouble . . .*

"We should send a message to the court anyway," the protocol mistress said shakily. "I'll figure out a way to make them listen to us. Surely nobody would argue when a girl's life is at stake."

"King Jerold is a stubborn man," the headmistress said hollowly. "And greedy. If he said he wants a new goldspinner, he's not going to listen till one arrives. He might not even listen after."

Della squeezed her eyes shut, stood on trembling legs, and forced herself to look up at the headmistress.

If this is my fault, she thought numbly, *then I have to be the one to solve it.*

"I might be able to speak with him," she croaked.

"You have the *spinning talent?*" Headmistress Riena demanded, her sharp eyes pinning Della.

"Not for sure!" Della shook her head, shaking. "I don't know for sure! But — my grandfather had it. Mom's kept that a secret since . . . since I was teensy . . ."

"How could you keep something like this from us?" the magic

mistress squealed. "Why, even the *possibility* of such a rare gift —"

"*Hush,*" the headmistress said, flicking a glare over at her. "Clearly Della didn't cherish the idea like you do."

"Yeah," Della said miserably. "Why can't the king just find an alchemist if he wants more gold?"

"Alchemy's notoriously unrealiable," the history mistress murmured. "No one's made a philosopher's stone in centuries."

"Besides, goldspinning has more mystique!" the magic mistress squeaked.

"Perhaps for a king," Della said bitterly. "Headmistress . . . how long do you think Aria's got before she dies from that spell?"

"Well . . ." The headmistress looked reluctant. "She's essentially in a coma, and she's very skinny. I don't think she'd digest anything but water. Perhaps . . . a week?"

"A *week?*" Della cried. "It's a three-day journey just to get to the castle from here!"

"All the more reason to run the test quickly!" the magic mistress cried, eyes gleaming. "There's no time to waste!"

"There's no call to rush her!" the headmistress barked. "We'll wait until she's ready."

Della took a deep breath, closed her eyes, and steeled her shoulders. "No. It's all right. If Aria's time is limited, the sooner we test me, the better. If I have the talent, I may have a chance to save her. If I don't . . . well, better to know quickly."

The magic mistress ran to fetch a spinning wheel. The headmistress picked up a pile of papers and shuffled through them, not seeming to want to look Della in the eye.

"A goldspinner . . ." she murmured. "I never dreamed we might have one in our midst."

It worked. Of course it worked. Three spins of the wheel, concentration, and a few magic words were all it took. Looking at the string of wire and the magic mistress's ecstacy, Della felt a wave of misery and relief.

I have a chance to save my roommate, she thought, closing her eyes. *But at what cost to me?*

"Goldspinner, goldspinner!" The fat king clapped his hands, his belly jiggling. "How fast are you? How high is your quality? Show me!"

Della fought to keep from glaring at him. "Fetch me a spinning wheel, sire, and I will do as you say."

The king waved his arms wildly at a pair of servants on the other end of the room. "Spinning wheel!" he hollered. "And lots of straw!"

Della scanned the room as thoroughly as she dared, but Prince Tendar was nowhere in sight. One snooty courtier stood in the corner, his arm around the waist of a sour-faced lady, but they looked like the crown prince and his newly-betrothed.

Where was Tendar? She had to find him as soon as possible. She had to get that ring back.

"So!" the king crowed, as four servants lugged in an enormous spinning wheel and six bales of hay, "prove your worth! Turn these all into gold!"

Della gaped at him. *"All?"*

"That's right!" The king rubbed his piggish hands together gleefully. *"All* of them!"

But that could take weeks! Della thought desperately. *Goldspinning works one straw, one thread, at a time — how can he expect me to do it all at once?*

Della's mind flew furiously, trying to think of an answer that wouldn't enrage the king.

"Have you ever seen a goldspinner in action, sire?" she burst out.

"Well." The king's brow wrinkled. "Not precisely."

"Well, that's because a . . . a goldspinner . . . needs privacy, sir." Della gulped. Would he buy it? Just one minute alone would let her sneak away and speak to Tendar . . . "We can't produce on demand without — um — while people are staring at us, and —"

"LOCK HER IN A DUNGEON!" the king howled. "If she can't produce gold from these by morning, kill her!"

"What?" Della gasped.

"Then you can *prove* you have the gift," the king leered. "See you in the morning!"

Della screamed and tried to run, but three of the king's servants grabbed her.

"And fill the dungeon with straw!" the king shouted. "I want to see all of it turned gold by morning!"

Della spun two long gold wires and then gave up in despair. Over an hour had passed, and the tiny threads looked worthless next to those giant mounds of straw. Besides, her fingers were sore and blistering.

Yesterday I was free, she thought, flinging a huge pile of straw at her spinning wheel. *I chose to come here to save my roommate. Now all that's going to happen is that we'll both die for nothing.*

"The universe is unfair!" Della shouted.

A shadow bubbled in front of her, and a hideous man slurped out of it.

"Agreed," he said.

"Who — what —?" Della gasped.

"A friend." The ugly man smirked. "Do you need help?"

"I don't — I can't — it's impossible!" Della gulped back tears that sprang to her eyes. "Even if you goldspin too, there's no way all this straw could turn by sunlight!"

"Sure there is." The man's face turned crafty. "Quite easily."

"How?" Della demanded, yanking a straw off her blouse and flinging it to the ground. "Even with a dozen goldspinners, this work would take weeks!"

The small man coughed. "Well, I am not, in fact, a goldspinner. But I *am* an alchemist. And I happen to have a philosopher's stone with me."

Della froze. "A philosopher's stone?" she whispered. "Aren't those nearly impossible to make?"

"Yes, nearly." The man smirked. "But I happen to be brilliant. Masterful. The greatest alchemist in hundreds of years —"

"Get to the point," Della muttered.

The man coughed. "Well. It so happens there's something you could do for me."

"I'm not marrying you," Della said flatly.

The man looked insulted. "Nothing like *that*. I just need a favor."

"I'm promising nothing about my first-born child!"

"Just a small favor!" the man shouted. "A teensy thing! You'll barely notice it!"

"What?" Della demanded.

"I . . . er . . ." The man coughed and looked away. "I'd rather not say . . . just yet."

"Then I'm not agreeing."

"Thankless, aren't you?" The ugly man eyed her. "Do you want your life saved or not?"

Della hesitated.

"Fine," the man said. "I'll just go back."

"All right!" Della shouted. "Help me!"

The man smirked. He reached into a shadow and pulled out a tiny gold ball. He tossed it in the air and caught it again.

"You get the straw," he told her. "I'll turn it. And let's hurry. We don't have much time left."

The king's fat jowls turned crimson at the sight of all the gold in the room. He wept with happiness as he flung himself into a huge pile of it.

His wife surveyed Della with a highly suspicious eye.

"None of that looks spun," she said, her mouth a thin line. "It's still shaped like straw."

"W-well, that can happen sometimes," Della stammered, her palms wet with fear as she held them behind her. "It — depends on the goldspinner, you see. Your majesties, may I . . . may I please see Prince Tendar? It's really urgent. You see —"

"Oh, certainly!" the king cried jubilantly, tossing handfuls of gold-straw in the air. "Whatever you wish!"

"*No.*" The queen shot him an angry glance. "I don't like this. There's something wrong. Besides, if she can turn one room of straw into gold, why can't she do another?"

The king froze, seeming stunned by that idea.

"N-no!" Della stammered. "I was — I've — I can only do so much at once! The magic's exhausted for now!"

The queen smiled thinly. "Well, you'd better hope it finds its way back soon, hadn't you? Guards, lock her up again. Let her sleep and eat. Then kill her if she isn't finished making more gold in the morning."

Della stared at the mounting piles of straw with mounting despair.

"Won't you let me out, please?" she pleaded to one of the strong-armed servants, lugging in hay. "Even for one minute? I'll pay you all the gold you want. No one would notice —"

"Nah." The servant shrugged. "Gold's going to be worthless if the king spends any of this. And he's bound to. Doesn't know the first thing about how economy works."

"I'll find some other way to pay you, then!" Della said desperately.

"Can't pay me if I'm dead," the servant smirked. "Face it, goldspinner — you're stuck here."

"But Prince Tendar!" Della cried as he left. "At least bring him here! I just need to talk to him for a minute!"

The servant burst out laughing.

"You and half the kingdom, missy!" he called, waving. "But you're not nearly luscious enough for his taste!"

Della slumped in the corner, staring at the endless straw that towered to the ceiling.

"Need help again?"

Della gasped, spinning around. "You!"

The little man pulled his arm from the shadow with a slight *slurp*. "For another favor, I could save you again."

"No way." Della smacked a handful of straw, which went flying. "If I change all this tonight, I'll just get stuck with more tomorrow. If I do it long enough, gold will become worthless, and the king will blame me. I'm dead either way."

The man considered, looking at her. "That's pretty accurate," he admitted.

Della closed her eyes and breathed in slowly. "I — I don't suppose you can take people with you when you're shadow-walking?"

"Welllll," the little man said slowly. "Maybe . . ."

"Yes or no."

"I've never tried it," the man muttered.

"Then let's try it." Della opened her eyes. "Take me out of here. Or at least to Prince Tendar. I need to speak with him."

"Prince Tendar?" The man looked stunned. "Why him?"

"None of your business!" Della shot back.

"Then I won't help you!"

"Then I won't live to do *your* favor!"

The man seemed struck by this.

"I mean, you do have a reason to keep me alive, don't you?" Della asked.

"Fine." The man looked surly. "I'll take you to Prince Tendar, then out of here. But after that, you have to do my favor."

"Only if you say what it is," Della said peevishly.

"It's a *small* favor," the man muttered, looking angry. "*Reasonable.*"

"Then tell me what it is!"

"Not till you've agreed!"

"That defeats the *purpose!*"

The man spun on his heel and folded his arms.

"*Huh!*" Della flopped onto the spinning wheel and sat there, waiting for him to change his mind.

Minutes passed. Silence.

Minutes more passed. Stony silence.

Every minute delayed is another minute lost of Aria's life, Della thought unwillingly.

"All right," she muttered. "You win. Once we leave, I'll do your favor."

"Promise?" the man asked eagerly.

"If I have to," Della muttered.

The man grinned and grabbed her arm. Della gasped as her body liquified. It felt like her whole self had turned into nausea.

They zipped up the wall outside the castle, around to a window, then right through it.

There, in a curtained bed, lay a beautiful prince. Asleep, he looked like an angel.

He's gorgeous, Della admitted, weak at the knees. *But he likes Aria,* she reminded herself quickly. *And really, that doesn't say much for his taste.*

"Here to give him a kiss?" the ugly man asked, smirking.

"Shut up," Della muttered. She walked over to the prince and put her hand on his mouth.

The prince's eyes flew open. "WHF—!"

He relaxed, catching sight of Della's face. She pulled her hand back slowly.

"Hel-lo, beautiful." The prince held out his arms. "Are you here for me?"

Outraged, Della smacked him.

"*Ow!*" the prince cried, clutching his jaw. "What was *that* for?"

"Aria's ring," Della hissed, checking over her shoulder for guards. One might arrive any minute. "Give it to me."

"What are you talking about?" The prince scrambled back, looking alarmed. "I don't have any ring!"

"*Aria's ring!*" Della hissed in a strangled shout. "Your *true love's* ring! She needs it to protect her from her birth-curse! Give it back!"

"I don't have a true love!" Prince Tendar scrambled back further, looking scared. "I've never had a true love! I don't want any ring!"

Della leaned forward. "Give — it — back," she hissed.

"GUARDS!" Tendar shouted, scrambling out of bed. "GUARDS! There are assassins in here! GUARDS!"

The door flew open. The ugly man lunged for Della, and they slurped into the shadows again.

Over walls. Through the doors. Faster, faster, away from the castle, through the forest, into wilds Della had never heard of before. Then, at last, they bubbled upwards again.

Della grasped a tree branch, dizzy. "That — has got to be — the most unpleasant way to travel," she gasped.

"But the fastest." The ugly man sat down. "If only at nighttime. You, ah . . . back there . . ."

"I — I failed." Della turned away, gripping the branch. "I totally failed. What's *wrong* with him? How could he pretend to have forgotten? *She's* spent the last few weeks obsessing!"

"Ah . . ." The ugly man sounded very awkward. "That . . . well, see, things . . ."

"I can't believe he's such a creep!" Della exploded. "He said she was his one-and-only! What a liar! What a *creep!*"

"He's . . . ah . . . well . . ." The man's voice fumbled. "You know . . . about that favor you said you'd do . . ."

"I've got to get that ring back," Della moaned. "I've *got* to get it back. But where's he *hiding* that thing?"

A lint-covered ring appeared under her nose. Della stared at it.

She turned around slowly.

"*You?*" she asked in a strangled voice. "*You — you —*"

"It was love at first sight!" the man cried piteously. "I'd never seen a maiden so enchanting!"

"SHE COULD DIE BECAUSE OF YOU!" Della shouted.

The man's eyes widened. "Die?"

"She's been in a coma for five days because she was missing that ring! She has a birth-curse! That was enchanted to protect her!"

"Here! Here!" The man dropped the ring in her hands. "Take it! Save her! She never said anything!"

Della snatched it. "How did you — *why* did you —"

"Just a whim." The small man looked away. Even his voice sounded red. "I'm good at magic. Sometimes I want to look handsome. Desired. Popular. So I use illusion. Then I met Aria."

"And the favor?" Della snarled.

The man pawed the ground with his foot. "I just . . . wanted somebody . . . to tell her the truth. Slowly. So she'd accept me. You're her friend. Her roommate. I thought, if anybody . . ."

Della closed her eyes, sighing. "Aria's shallow. All the clever lead-ins, all the careful explaining, won't make her accept you. Her 'true love' was the prince you pretended to be."

"But if you just explain —" the man said desperately. "The real me —"

"She'd see nothing in the real you."

The man stumbled back. "But I'm *brilliant!*" he snarled. "I'm a *genius! I invented* shadow-walking! I created a philosopher's stone! I could give her *anything —*"

"EXCEPT POPULARITY!" Della shouted. "Brilliant magician you may be, but you're a *dunce* socially!"

The man's shoulders slumped. He turned away.

Della closed her eyes.

Harsh tongue, she thought. *Harsh words. Mother would whip me.*

"I'm sorry," she said quietly. "But it's the truth."

"I'll take you back," the man said dully, without turning around. "You save her. It's the least I can do, if she's dying."

Aria's eyes opened slowly, looking into Della's face and yawning widely.

"Hello, Delly," she chirped. "I feel *marrrrrvelously* well-rested today!"

"I'm glad to hear it," Della muttered. "You almost died."

"Oh, don't be so *dramatic!*" Aria giggled, slapping her arm. "Delly, you think everything's life-or-death, *seriously!*"

"Ask anyone," Della snarled. "You've been asleep five and a half days. Your birth-curse nearly killed you. I had to get that ring back from your 'true love' in order to save you."

Aria stared at her blankly. She lifted her hand to her face and peered at the ring.

"Then where's Tendar?" she asked tremulously. "Why'd you wake me? He should have done it. He should have kissed me. Tendy?"

"Right here," a voice said dully.

Aria peered around her roommate's shoulder and screamed.

"MONSTER!" she shrieked. "MONSTER! DELLY!"

Della slapped her.

Aria gasped, clutching her cheek.

"He's the one you fell in love with," Della snarled. "He made himself look like Tendar so you'd fall for him, too. But he has plenty of other qualities. He's a genius —"

"Stop it!" Aria sobbed. "Stop lying! I don't want some stupid genius! I want Tendy!"

Della stood up, slowly, struggling with her fury.

"I wrecked my life for you," she said coldly. "The king will kill me if he ever finds me. I'll live in hiding for the rest of my life. And I did it for you. The least you can do is listen to him."

Aria hesitated and peeked over Della's shoulder again. She yelped, dove under her covers, and shook her head.

"Nooooo!" she cried. "No, no! He's too ugly!"

Della's face turned hot with fury.

"It's all right." The man's voice sounded wooden. "Everyone hates me. Everyone rejects me. Why should she be any different?"

"Because she claimed she loved you," Della snapped.

"Doesn't matter." The man's eyes looked dead. "It was based on lies anyway."

Something in his voice scared Della. *He might do something drastic now,* she realized.

"I don't care what you look like," she blurted out. "I mean, yes, you're hardly pretty. But I'm an outlaw too, you realize. That makes us equals."

Slowly, the man looked up at her.

"You're brilliant," Della said, swallowing. *Oh, how ugly he looks. But that doesn't matter. Or at least it shouldn't. I can't let it matter. I can't.* "All I ever wanted was an education. If we stayed together . . . would you teach me?"

The man stared at her. Fear and hope and anger flitted across his face.

"You feel sorry for me," he accused her.

Della looked down. She couldn't deny it.

"But I also feel sorry for *me*," she insisted. "I'm dead if the king finds me, and you're the only person who'd be able to keep me safe. As for you . . . well . . . I can't offer love, but I can offer companionship. Better than loneliness."

There was silence a long moment.

"You mean we could be friends."

"Yes," Della said quietly. "We could be friends."

Slowly, the man held out his hand.

"All right," he muttered. "Friends."

They slurped into the shadows. There was silence.

"Does this mean I need a new roommate, Delly?" Aria cried from under the sheet.

Unicess

Elysia was the only one of her friends to not have wings yet. Even Renae, who was six months younger than her, had grown hers in. But Elysia's hadn't arrived yet.

"There was a scratchy spot between my shoulderblades," Renae had explained eagerly, three days after the wings had sprouted, "and they were growing in the next morning. I'll be able to fly in just another week!"

Papa had promised Elysia that she'd grow her wings soon. But it hadn't happened yet.

Elysia stared out the window, glumly watching Renae. Now that she had wings, Renae could play with all the older kids, instead of watching the babies, like Elysia still had to. If Elysia tried to go outside to play, she'd get stuck baby-sitting again for sure. Parents always wanted older kids near the younger ones, to make sure they stayed safe. And if the older kids didn't have wings yet, either, all the better — they wouldn't be tempted to go off playing with friends.

"I'm the oldest person in the whole village not to have wings," Elysia muttered to herself, staring at the others jealously. "I'm the only one my age who can't play buzz tag with the others. It isn't fair!"

Elysia had a dream that night. At least, she thought it was a dream — but afterwards, she wasn't certain. It had felt too real to be a dream, but it couldn't have been real. Could it?

She dreamt she woke up in the middle of the night, because she heard a noise outside. Then she went to the window, the same window she'd been looking out the day before, and there was a unicess waiting for her.

Elysia's breath caught in her throat. She stared at the creature, the winged unicorn, with something like awe. She knew it was a unicess, because she'd heard about them in stories, but she'd never thought they existed.

Come with me, the unicess said.

Swallowing, Elysia climbed out of the window, onto the grass outside. The unicess stared at her for a long moment. Then it spoke again.

Climb onto my back.

Elysia stared at the unicess with wide eyes. But something in the creature's gaze told her she had to obey. So she hauled herself up, barely avoiding the feathery wings, and tried to figure out what she was supposed to do now.

Hold on.

And then came the part of their journey that Elysia was sure had to be a dream. They flew up, up higher than any human could fly, above the part of the sky where you should be able to breathe. Then they reached something that looked like a cave, only it was made of crystal. The unicess landed on a ledge right near the cave's opening, and ordered her to dismount.

And follow me, the unicess added, heading towards the gaping maw.

Frightening as the cave looked like it might be, Elysia didn't dare disobey. What would she do here without the unicess, anyway? And anyway, if this was a dream, she couldn't get hurt.

Could she?

The crystalline walls loomed up around her, sharp and cold and unyielding. She shivered, rubbing her arms, as she followed the unicess down a long corridor. The creature's hooves *tink*ed against the crystal floor with each step it took, making a regular rhythm that began to pound into Elysia's mind. *Tink, tink, tink.* At least the cave wasn't as dark as she'd feared it might be — the walls seemed to give off some kind of light, so she never lost sight of where they were going.

Finally, they reached a huge chamber with some kind of fountain in the middle of it. Elysia rubbed her eyes, not knowing if she was seeing it for real, but the fountain was still there when she looked again. The water in it seemed to glow with an eerie quality, a light that had nothing to do with the reflected walls or crystals.

"What is it?" she whispered.

The unicess stared back. Elysia thought she caught a hint of amusement in the creature's eyes. *The flight water,* it answered. *Your kind was not originally born with wings. Nor was mine. Both of us gained the gift of flight through this water. But my kind, who live longer and in greater heights than yours, have not forgotten where our wings came from, nor where the flight water still resides. Yours have.*

Elysia stared at the unicess. "You mean — the people of my village?"

Yes. Twice now we unicorns have had to interfere. Once in a century, a person of your village without wings must come here to drink the flight water again. If no one comes, children will stop growing wings, and eventually, winged humans will disappear completely. Do you want that to happen?

Elysia stared at the unicess in horror. "Oh, no!" she cried. "Life would be awful if no one could fly!"

Then go to the fountain. If you are pure in heart, it will allow you to drink. And if you do, it will allow your people to keep the gift of flight for another hundred years.

"And give me wings too?" Elysia asked, hardly daring hope.

Yes.

Elysia bit her lip, frightened, but also tingling inside with excitement. She was going to gain wings of her own at last! And do something to help the rest of her people, too. Even if she was jealous of them, she'd never wish them harm.

She stepped forward, and knelt down by the pool of water. In its smooth surface, she could see her reflection shining back at her. Then the water rippled of its own accord, and her face vanished, replaced with a brightness so dazzling, it hurt her eyes.

She turned back to the unicess, blinking at the spots that had appeared in front of her vision. "What does that mean?" she asked anxiously. "Is it good?"

Yes. It means you have been judged worthy. Drink.

Elysia turned back to the pool, squinting as she looked at the water. Then she closed her eyes, lowered her face to the water, and drank.

A cold shiver ran down her spine, and when she pulled back, the pool had stopped glowing. The light of the crystals around them seemed to be growing dim, as well.

Quickly, the unicess said, its voice sounding urgent now. *We must leave soon, before the light vanishes. Climb onto my back again.*

Feeling strangely tingly, Elysia obeyed. Then the unicess set off down the passageway they had come through at a gallop, hooves hitting the crystal with a tinkling clatter that sounded like a cross between gravel falling on glass, and raindrops hitting a window.

Sooner than she expected, she and the unicess were out of the caves again. Then they were flying down towards her village, and before Elysia knew it, they were back at her home again. She pulled away from the unicess with a little reluctance, sure she would never see the creature again, and then climbed back through her window.

Sure enough, by the time she had gotten back in bed, the unicess was gone.

And when Elysia woke up again, she was certain it had been a dream.

Except for one thing — the tingling feeling she'd felt from the pool was still with her when she woke up. And her shoulderblades were starting to itch.

As if her wings were about to sprout.

Cindy's Fairy Godmother

Mother gave me an encouraging smile as she gestured at the ancient-looking woman standing next to her. "Cindy, there's someone I'd like you to meet."

I scrutinized the old lady. She was probably a visiting dignitary, but I couldn't remember ever seeing her before. "Who is she?"

A small laughed escaped Mother. "Your fairy godmother. I'm surprised you didn't recognize her."

I remembered her now. She was that old lady who used to visit when I was five or six. "Why didn't she come before?"

My fairy godmother caught me with her beady eyes. "I was busy," she said waspishly. "A pleasure to see you too, Cinderella."

I scowled. "Cindy. Mother's Cinderella."

"Do forgive me." I caught a sarcastic glint in her eyes, and it annoyed me. "I suppose you're wondering why I'm here?"

I shrugged, though I was dying of curiosity. "I don't care."

A mocking smile appeared on her lips. "Same reason I came to her mother when she was twelve. Don't suppose you'd be interested?"

I reluctantly confessed to a teeny spark of interest.

Her eyes glinted. "Just after her father died. I came to grant her her one or three."

She was baiting me, but I had to ask. "One or three what?"

The mocking smile widened. "Wishes. Which would you prefer?"

"Wishes?" I stammered. My eyes must have widened. "Real wishes?"

"One or three." The old fairy seemed to be enjoying herself. "Take your pick."

That didn't seem a difficult choice to me, unless there was something else I didn't know. "What's the catch?"

"Very good. Your father's daughter too, I see." My fairy godmother pulled four ribbons from a pocket I hadn't seen before. She held the white one in her right hand, and the others in her left. "The one wish lasts permanently. The other three end at midnight."

A flash of inspiration came to me. "The balls! The ones where Mother met Father! That was *you?*"

"Very good." I detected a hint of a sneer on her lips. "Now choose."

It wasn't an easy decision. "Can I think about it first?"

She thrust the ribbons at me. "Think later. Choose now."

"You will have all four, eventually," Mother offered, glancing at my fairy godmother. "You gain the one or three later, at eighteen." She gave me an encouraging smile. "I chose the one first, but you're welcome to choose either."

I hesitated, but the old fairy shoved the ribbons in my face.

"Choose now. Choose, or lose them all."

Afraid she would make good on the threat, I reached out a hand and touched the hand with the three ribbons. I turned to Mother with a questioning look on my face.

She said nothing, so I let the ribbons fall into my palm.

"Done!" my fairy godmother cackled. "Your first wish has to be made tonight. The second comes tomorrow, the third the day after. Skip a day, and you lose a wish." She gave me an unpleasant smile. "Understand?"

I wanted to scowl at her, but thought better of it. "I understand."

Invisibility was the best wish I could think of for the first day. I had a lot of fun sneaking up on people and making them think the castle was haunted, but that got boring after awhile. I focused on Ellen, my governess, for an hour and nearly had her in hysterics before Mother thought to tell her about my wishes and apparent invisibility.

I didn't have as much fun with her after that. Every time Ellen heard my voice, she started lecturing, and I couldn't even filch desserts from the kitchen after Ellen talked to the cooks. At least Ellen couldn't trap me in any of her lectures; I snuck off whenever she started one.

I had fun teasing the crocodiles in the moat, but Ellen put a stop to that as soon as she realized the stick poking at them was mine. By that time, I was tired of being invisible anyway, so I let her march me inside and try to give me another lecture.

My mind was too busy to pay a drop of attention, though. By the end of the lecture, I knew exactly what I wanted to do with my next wish. The crocodiles had given me the idea.

I held up the yellow ribbon. "I wish to be able to breathe water!"

The red ribbon had disappeared when I wished to be invisible, so I was a little disappointed when this one didn't. I was about to repeat my wish when I heard my fairy godmother's voice.

"Breathe water or breathe *in* water?"

I was so startled, I dropped the ribbon. After a moment, I recovered the courage to pick it up again. "What's the difference?"

The voice sounded grouchy. "Vast. Breathing water requires changing your entire respiratory system. Breathing *in* water requires making a simple addition. Which do you want?"

I was starting to have second thoughts about my second wish. "Maybe I'll wish for something else."

The voice sounded triumphant now. "Oh, no you don't. You made your wish, now choose."

I shrugged, considerably irked. "Breathing *in* water, I guess. But I want to be in water when the wish starts."

I thought I heard the fairy mumbling under her breath, but she did it. The next thing I knew, I was staring into a blurry mess of wetness. I choked when I tried to open my mouth, but I breathed fine when I kept it closed. The only problem was, I had to hold my nose to keep water from going up it and making it itch.

I may have been able to breathe underwater, but I couldn't see very well. I think I passed some interesting fish, but it was hard to be sure. I was sick of the wish in no time at all, but I still had several wet and miserable hours left to go.

My third wish had to be a good one. I thought and thought, but nothing occured to me until breakfast the next morning. I looked across the table at Mother, and I knew what I wanted my wish to be. It was a brilliant wish, but I wouldn't tell anyone about it, even Mother. She'd probably figure it out on her own, like she had with the invisibility.

I certainly didn't tell Ellen when she tried to demand my plans for the day. It would serve her right if she thought I'd gone invisible again.

In the privacy of my room, I held up the blue ribbon. "I wish to visit Mother when she was my age!"

I shouldn't have been surprised when the third ribbon spoke, but I hadn't been expecting it. At least I didn't drop it this time.

"Do you have any *idea* how difficult time travel is?"

I felt a perverse satisfaction at annoying my fairy godmother. I certainly didn't know anyone who deserved it more, except Ellen and Grandma Morgana. "That's my wish."

I think the ribbon growled. The next thing I knew, the scenery around me dissolved, and I was standing in a grand home. Nowhere near as grand as our castle, but much more ornate.

"And make sure that grate *stays* clean!"

My eyes widened as I recognized Grandma Morgana's voice. I should have remembered she would be here. I managed to hide behind a drapery just in time.

When she entered the room, dragging Mother, she screamed a tongue-lashing Ellen would have coveted. Mother looked like she was going to cry. She kept trying to say she *had* cleaned the grate, but Grandma Morgana wouldn't listen. I think she would have scolded a lot longer if the butler hadn't shown up and said there was someone there to see Aunt Agatha.

Grandma Morgana swept from the room, and Mother bent slowly to clean the grate again. Indignation shot through me. Mother wasn't a servant! She was a *queen*.

I was about to venture from my hiding place when Aunt

Agatha pounded down the stairs. With that familiar sour-apple expression, that ugly girl couldn't have been anything but a younger, thinner, whinier version of Aunt Agatha. A scowl crossed her face as she caught sight of Mother.

"Mama! You *can't* let the Cindersoot downstairs when we have company!" Aunt Agatha stormed towards the room I could only assume was the parlor. "You have no idea what a *humiliation* — oh, Auguste!" Her tone changed abruptly, becoming syrupy-sweet. "What a pleasant surprise!"

I breathed a sigh of relief as Aunt Agatha disappeared from sight, and slipped out of the curtains.

Mother squeaked in surprise when she saw me. "Who are you?"

I smiled nervously, hoping I looked friendly. "I'm Cindy."

A frightened look flitted across her face. "If my stepmother catches you here, we'll both be in trouble. Are you one of Cook's nieces?"

I repressed a shudder at the thought. "I came to see you."

Her eyes widened in disbelief. "Me?" She scrubbed her eyes, and I realized they were red from crying. That made me feel awfully awkward. I hadn't known Mother used to cry. "My stepmother hasn't let anyone come to see me, not since Papa died —"

She took a deep breath, and I realized she was trying to stop herself from crying. I jumped in before she could start.

"Your fairy godmother'll make everything better."

Mother looked confused now, and a little disbelieving. "I don't have a godmother."

"Yes, you do, and she's a fairy. She's mine too, and she'll grant you a wish, and you'll be happier. Honest."

Mother opened her mouth to reply, but Grandma Morgana stormed in before she could.

The result was catastrophic. I was thrown out of the house, and I didn't dare try to get in after the butler caught me on my third attempt. In the end, I wandered through the streets, wishing I could walk in the castle gardens instead. When night fell, it was freezing, and I shivered in my thin dress as I tried to doze off in the bushes near the house.

For the third time in three days, I was relieved when I woke up to find my wish over. But this time, I didn't have a new wish to replace it.

I ate my breakfast listlessly. I'd wasted all three wishes, and none of them had been much fun. What kind of a wisher was I, anyway? At this rate, I'd be miserable when I made my one.

Ellen was visiting her sister, the only consolation I could see about the day. I brightened when Mother offered to take me for a walk through the gardens. I wanted to talk to her about my wishes, but I didn't know how to begin.

Halfway through the rose arches, I managed to summon my courage. "Mother, did you really use all three of your wishes to go to a ball?"

Mother laughed softly. "Three balls, one after the other. I couldn't think of a better use for the first one, and after that — well, I'll admit to wanting to see the prince again. He was attracted to my unfeigned interest, and I fell in love with his charm from the start."

I nodded. I'd heard the story. "What happened after that?"

"He searched me out and we ended up getting married. You know the rest."

I felt stubbornness rising in me. "No, I don't. I don't know what you used your one wish for."

Mother didn't respond for a long time. Her eyes focused on something far away, and I got the impression she was remembering something. Finally, she spoke.

"I suppose I can tell you now. You were the one who gave me the idea, Cindy."

I gave her a quizzical look. "I thought you made the wish before you even met Father."

Mother nodded, and I suddenly realized what she meant.

"You don't mean yesterday? When I went to the past and — and —"

Mother nodded again, and I felt my eyes widening.

"What did you wish for?"

"The wisest wish I think I could have ever made."

"What? What?"

She smiled. "Happiness."

I repeated the word in disbelief. "*Happiness?* But that's so — so ordinary!"

"Happiness." Her voice was firm, and I realized she'd never regretted her permanent wish. "Happiness, no matter what my situation. Happiness, which I had precious little of after my father's death. Plain, ordinary happiness."

And we turned and headed back to the castle.

Monster Under the Bed

"Goodnight, sweetie." Jennifer's mother tucked her in and switched out the light. "Don't you dare get out of bed."

"Night, Mommy," Jennifer said sleepily.

Her mother nodded and closed the door. Jennifer listened for the quiet *click* and the soft *thud* of footsteps going down the stairs.

She leaned over the edge of the bed. "Monster!" she called softly. "Monster under the bed! Where are you?"

Slowly, a voice grumbled from beneath her. "Where I always am."

"I thought you might have gone away," Jennifer said accusingly. "You didn't even try to grab my ankles when I got into bed."

"Light was too bright."

"Don't be silly." Jennifer leaned over further, her head almost level with the floor. "You've tried before in more light." She giggled. "You still haven't gotten me."

The monster grunted.

"What happens when you get someone?" Jennifer demanded, pulling her head up a little. "You never told me."

"Power," the monster grunted. "Got power over the person, if they believe in me."

Jennifer pondered that for a moment. "What kind of power?"

"Never done it. Don't know."

"You won't ever," Jennifer grinned, pulling herself back up on top of her bed. "I'm too fast for you."

"Get you someday."

"No, you won't," Jennifer said cheerfully.

The monster grunted again.

Jennifer scowled. "You're being boring today. You're supposed to argue with me."

"Don't feel like it." The monster sounded sullen now.

Jennifer leaned over her bed again, curious. "Why? What happened?"

The monster's voice came mumbling from under the bed. "Her, if you must know."

"Her?" Jennifer repeated, perplexed. "Who?"

"*Her*," the monster repeated with a growl. "The one who was in here."

Jennifer's brow wrinkled. "Mommy?"

"No. The one before her."

Jennifer's face cleared. "Oh! You mean David's new girlfriend!" She giggled. "She's Cynda, and she's really nice. She gave me a bag of M&Ms just for promising I wouldn't tell Mommy about that movie she and David rented and watched in the family room while Mommy and Daddy were gone."

The monster grunted noncommittally.

"Have you ever tried M&Ms?"

"What's M&Ms?" the monster asked suspiciously.

"You'll love it," Jennifer promised, pulling herself back up into bed and feeling around on her bedside table for the bag. "I still have some. Try one." She tossed an M&M in the general direction of the floor. She heard a *chink* as it hit the wood floor, and a soft *shush* as the monster grabbed it.

"What is it?" he asked doubtfully.

"It's an *M&M*," Jennifer said, exasperated.

"What do you do with it?"

"You eat it, silly. I'll show you." She grabbed an M&M and shoved it in her mouth.

"Can't see without light," the monster grumbled from under the bed. "Hate light. And don't eat hard things."

"Don't you eat?"

"'Course I do." The monster sounded a little irritated. "Eat dust."

"Yuck." Jennifer wrinkled her nose. "I like M&Ms better."

"Tastes good."

Jennifer wrinkled her nose again. "Mommy says dust has to be cleaned out all the time."

"Don't like it when you do that," the monster grumbled. "Too bright, then have to start growing the dust all over again."

"Mommy says it's dirty when you don't," Jennifer said loyally.

"Not dirty," the monster said sullenly. "Just hungry."

"Then eat something else."

"Can't."

"Why not?"

The monster sounded stubborn. "Can't."

Jennifer sighed loudly. She knew how stubborn the monster could be.

"Don't like *her*," the monster said again, louder.

"Cynda?"

"*Her.*"

"I like her." Jennifer gulped down her last handful of M&Ms. "She's nice."

"Don't." The monster sounded sullen again. "Don't like exterminators."

Jennifer put the now-empty bag on her nightstand and wriggled back under her sheets. "But they make icky bugs go away."

"Other exterminators. Ones that make *us* go away."

Jennifer stopped wriggling, startled. "They make monsters go away?"

The monster mumbled an indistinct answer.

Jennifer stared out into the darkness. She didn't want anyone to make her monster go away. "Maybe you're wrong," she said doubtfully.

"Know an exterminator when I see one."

Jennifer shivered and wriggled further under the covers.

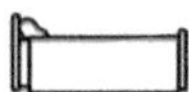

"Oh, no!"

Jennifer looked up from her coloring book. "What's wrong, Mommy?"

Her mother was talking on the phone. Jennifer made a face and grabbed another crayon. Cerulean blue, this time. Next to the Purple Mountain Majesty on the princess's dress.

"Yes — oh, I'm sorry, Hilary. What a nightmare — yes — of course I understand, it's just — yes, of course — yes. All right. I'm sorry too. Goodnight, Hilary."

Jennifer looked up as her mother hung up the phone. "What happened to Hilary?"

Her mother ran her hand nervously through her hair. "Hilary just canceled."

Jennifer brightened. "So I can stay here by myself?"

"No!" Jennifer's mother took a deep breath. "No, Jennifer. We'll just have to find someone else."

Jennifer scowled. "I'm old enough."

"You most certainly are not. Do you know where I put Serena's number?"

Jennifer opened her mouth to complain, but the front door slammed before she could.

". . . down here, I'll just be a sec." Jennifer heard her older brother pound up the stairs. He sounded like an elephant.

Cynda came sauntering into the kitchen. Jennifer drew back from her slightly, not sure what to think.

Cynda saw her and beamed. "Jennifer! How good to see you again!"

Jennifer scowled. That smile made her look like a crocodile. "Fine."

"Yes, I understand — all right." Jennifer's mother hung up the phone for a second time. "That was Serena. She can't come ei— oh, Cynda! When did you come in?"

Cynda's crocodile smile widened slightly. "Just a moment ago. Were you having some kind of problem?"

"Oh, baby-sitters." Jennifer's mother ran a hand through her hair again. "Hilary canceled at the last moment, and Serena's not available either — you know Fridays — we're just going to have to cancel our dinner reservations, I suppose —"

"I'm old enough —" Jennifer protested.

"Jennifer, *anyone* who still thinks she has a monster under her bed —"

Cynda's eyebrows raised the slightest fraction of an inch. "A monster?"

"Her imaginary friend," Jennifer's mother explained vaguely. "Can you remember where I put Kim's number?"

"I'm free tonight."

Jennifer's mother stared at Cynda, her eyes widening as if Christmas had come three months early. "Don't you and David have something planned?"

"Just a basketball game." Cynda smiled that crocodile smile again. "I'm not a cheerleader. I think he'll forgive me if I skip this once."

A look of relief crossed Jennifer's mother's face. "Well then, if you're sure — we'll pay you, of course, six dollars an hour —"

Cynda's smile widened. "I'll look forward to it."

Jennifer's skin prickled in apprehension. She had a bad feeling about this.

"Monopoly? Risk? Candy Land?"

Jennifer faked a yawn. "I think I want to go to bed."

"At eight o'clock?" Cynda's eyebrows arched. "Most children your age would be begging to stay up."

Jennifer yawned again, as widely as she could. "I'm tired." She got up. "I want to go to bed."

Cynda grabbed her arm. "Didn't you sleep well last night? Why not?"

Jennifer tried to pull her arm away, but Cynda wouldn't let her. "I'm just tired," she said defensively.

Cynda nodded wisely. "I understand, Jennifer, but it's nothing to be ashamed of. I was afraid of monsters when I was your age."

Jennifer wrenched her arm free and scowled. "I'm not scared of monsters."

Cynda smiled sweetly. "Of course you're not — that's what children always *claim*. But I know better. You have a real one, don't you?"

Jennifer folded her arms across her chest. "Real what?"

"Monster under your bed." Cynda smiled that crocodile smile again.

Jennifer scowled. "No."

Cynda laughed. It wasn't a nice laugh. "What would you say if I told you I could get rid of it?"

Jennifer stamped her foot, furious. "I'd say you're a bad person and should leave other people's monsters alone!"

"Now, Jennifer," Cynda said soothingly, an eyebrow arching, "I understand you think you can solve the problem yourself. I thought the same thing when I was a child, but it doesn't work that way. You have to find someone *trained* to do it. Someone with the proper tools. Someone —"

"I don't want an exterminator!"

Cynda looked a little startled, then smiled. "So you even know the term for it. So much the better. Now let's go upstairs and get rid of your monster." She patted the bag she carried everywhere with her. "I have everything I need right here."

Jennifer backed away, her heart beating rapidly. "No!"

Cynda shook her head sadly. "Really, Jennifer, you need my help, whether or not you're willing to admit —"

Jennifer dashed for the stairs. She made it to her bedroom and locked the door before Cynda could follow her. Panting, she knelt down by the bed.

"Monster!" she hissed. "Monster! Cynda's coming up, she's going to exterminate you! Do something, quick!"

The growly voice emerged as Cynda pounded on the door. "Can't do anything."

"Jennifer! Let me in right now!"

"Quick, quick, *quick*," Jennifer wailed. "I don't want her here!"

"Can't do anything," the monster repeated dully. "Shouldn't've let her in."

"I didn't — Mommy did!"

"If you don't let me in," Cynda threatened, "I *will* come in on my own. I know how to pick locks."

"*Do* something," Jennifer cried desperately. "Anything!"

The monster pondered as the doorknob clicked and turned, and Cynda stepped into the room. She stood silhouetted in the doorway, until her hand reached out and clicked the light on.

Jennifer jumped in front of her bed, shielding it from the exterminator. "Go away! Leave my monster alone!"

"You silly girl." Cynda sounded annoyed now. "You don't know what you're asking for. Get out of my way."

"No."

Cynda shoved her aside. Jennifer jumped back and pulled at her arm, unsuccessfully. Cynda slapped her away and —

The monster's hand fastened around her ankle.

"Got one," the monster said slowly, triumphantly. "Told you. Could do it if wanted to."

Cynda screamed in revulsion and tried to kick the monster's hand. Jennifer grabbed her bag, and she and Cynda played a furious game of tug-of-war. Cynda was much stronger.

"Monster! Monster! Get them both!" Jennifer yelled.

"Both?" the monster repeated slowly.

"Ankles!"

"Oh." The monster's slow, pondering voice came from under the bed. "Why?"

"So you'll have power over her!"

Cynda snatched the bag from Jennifer, panting heavily. "Don't you dare do that again," she hissed, and started to open the bag —

But a strange, dreamlike expression drifted across her face before she could.

Jennifer saw her chance and snatched the bag back. She looked for a place to hide it, and finally buried it in her trash, under several old homework assignments. When she turned back, Cynda was still frozen, the monster's hands wrapped around her ankles.

"Do something with her."

"Hard to hold on to," the monster mumbled.

"Do something with her!"

"Don't know what."

Jennifer's eyes narrowed. "Make her stop believing in monsters."

"Don't know how."

"Yes, you do."

The monster sounded unhappy. "Don't want to let go. Make her forget, have to let go."

Jennifer stamped her foot. "She wants to exterminate you!"

The monster pondered that for a moment. Then, slowly, it pulled its hands away.

"Strangest child I've ever sat for," Cynda was telling David as Jennifer snuck behind the couch. "First, she *volunteers* to go to bed at eight o'clock."

David laughed and picked up the remote control. "My sister's weird. You gotta respect that."

"Then she yells at me to turn the hall light off, because it's scaring the monster under her bed," Cynda continued, ticking the points off on her fingers.

Jennifer scooped up a handful of dust. That ought to be just enough to start a new farm under her bed. Then the monster wouldn't complain about not getting enough to eat.

"Then she comes downstairs at nine thirty to complain she can't sleep and wants to know if she can have a glass of water. So I go to the kitchen to get her one, and I come up, and she's talking to thin air!"

"Monster under the bed," David grinned, flipping through a few channels. "She does that all the time. I think she really believes in that thing."

Cynda rolled her eyes, looking exasperated. "But it's so *stupid*. Everyone knows monsters don't exist."

David shrugged. "So it's an imaginary friend. So what?"

Cynda groaned and shook her head. "I'm beginning to think your whole family's strange."

Jennifer snuck out from behind the couch and headed up to her room, grinning triumphantly.

Time Switch

"Cordie! Cordie!"

Saylie heard the voice behind her, but ignored it.

"Cordie!"

I'm home. Saylie's eyes ran hungrily over the highrises in her neighborhood. She'd woken up this morning, just as she had for the last three months in 1923 — and she was back.

Home. In 2083.

It didn't look the same as she remembered. Saylie sighed, rubbing her eyes. So three months had passed here, as well as back there. She might have figured. She'd thought, since the tri-vids always showed no time passing at all when you got back from time-travel, that she might get lucky . . .

A hand grabbed her shoulder. Saylie screamed in surprise.

"Cordie, come on! Don't ignore me!"

Saylie whirled around. The girl staring at her was completely unfamiliar.

A horrible seed of doubt woke in her.

What did I change? she thought, frightened. *I thought I was careful. Did I mess something up? Did I change my own name?*

"Who's Cordie?" she blurted out.

Bafflement flashed across the girl's face. "You are. Cordelia Langley —"

The girl stopped and gasped.

"Oh, no! You're Saylie!"

"Who else would I be?" Saylie cried.

The girl smiled awkwardly. "Well, it's just . . . I mean, I guess you've never met me . . . I'm Karen . . . see, I made friends with Cordie . . ."

"Who's Cordie?" Saylie shouted.

"She was you!" the stranger said, looking hurt. "Weren't you her, I mean, didn't the two of you switch places? Isn't that how it works?"

"Apparently not," Saylie said flatly.

Karen stared at her. "But . . . she was you . . . and now you're right back in your body again . . . I mean, you *did* go somewhere, didn't you?"

Saylie was silent.

Karen looked nervous. "Well, didn't you?!"

Saylie hesitated. "I —"

"You did!" Karen breathed out. "I knew it was a time switch!"

"I don't know what a 'time switch' is," Saylie said tightly, "but when I was stuck in the past, I wasn't 'Cordie.' I lived the life of a girl named Katherine."

Karen stared at her.

"In 1923," Saylie added.

Karen ran her hand through her hair, looking lost. "Cordie lived in 1763. England. Her parents had been considering moving out here before she left. She couldn't believe it when I told her about the revolution."

Saylie shook her head, feeling lost.

"There was a legend in her family," Karen said tentatively. "The time switch, I mean. She told me about it. It's said some people in their family have the ability to use it once in their lives —"

"Three-way," Saylie murmured. "It must have been three-way at least. Somehow, someone messed things up, and made it three-way at least."

Karen shivered. "Then we have no idea who did it?"

"My money's on Cordie," Saylie muttered. "Since she knew so much about this in the first place."

"Or maybe some fourth person," Karen said glumly. "Who knows how many people got involved here?"

Cordelia woke slowly. Something felt wrong.

It was too quiet, she realized. Nothing was humming. No dream-recorder. No alarm clock. No visiphone.

Hope pounded in her heart. Was she — dare she hope — home?

Cordie sat up quickly, blinking in the dim light of sunrise. The furniture around her swam into view, familiar and comforting as ever.

Home again.

Except . . .

What was this room? Had her family *moved* while she was gone?

What had Saylie *done* in her place?

Catherine flung the sheet off her bed and punched the air triumphantly.

1923. She was definitely back in 1923. But she was definitely *not* home.

The smell of pancakes, not soggy biscuits, floated up the stairs. Catherine sniffed appreciatively. Then she sank back into her bed, basking in the feeling of her total success.

Grandfather used to talk about the time switch when she was a child. After he died, she'd found his old diaries. Read about the way he'd done one himself. That was when she knew — she just *knew* — she'd be able to use one herself someday.

And speaking of journals . . .

Catherine rooted through the nightstand by her bed and found a small hardback book. She ripped it open and flipped through the pages, hoping, hoping.

Yes! Her future descendent had written in it. Hints of the future to come, hints Catherine could keep. She clutched the journal, grinning like crazy. This would be the key to her wealth and happiness. This was why she'd twisted the time switch to make it three-way.

Only one chance in a lifetime, she thought dreamily, swinging her feet over the edge of her bed. *And I got the best of both worlds. Future knowledge, and changing my own family's past. Now Dad won't get shot by that stupid hunting rifle, and Mum won't go on and on about my taste for American music.*

Catherine giggled and put the journal away. She hopped to the door and peeked out.

Katherine's Room. Stay out, a sign on front said.

Catherine blinked at that.

I spell it with a K now?

Oh, well. She could always change it back.

After all, from now on, everything was going her way.

The Apple of Discrd

I picked up the golden apple. It felt cool to the touch, even in the hot morning sun.

I knew it, I thought. *I knew it was magical.*

"Is this what you saw?" I asked Cassandra.

She shivered and backed away.

I gripped the apple. This was why I was here. This was why I had gone straight to see Cassandra. I knew she could find it for me. "Let's destroy it," I said.

"*No!*" Cassandra yelped, seizing my arm. "You can't! The Fates —!"

I stared at her, astonished. "You dreamed your entire nation was going to die if your brother finds this. And you're worried about the *Fates?*"

"I've angered a god before," Cassandra muttered. "It doesn't pay."

"You had every right to refuse Apollo," I began heatedly.

"Men hold women as slaves," she snapped. "Gods hold mortals as slaves. Fates hold everybody as slaves. It is the way of things."

She pried the apple from my hands and plonked it back on the grass.

"And as you are *my* family's slave," she added sharply, "you will do as I say."

I decided that I did not like Cassandra.

I was not, in fact, King Priam's slave. I was not even a mortal. I had been a guest at Peleus's wedding, which my sister had planned. And I'd watched the apple create jealousy and rage within every goddess present.

I made myself invisible and waited until Cassandra had forgotten me. Then I returned to my mortal guise and snuck back to the orchard. The apple lay there, glinting in the morning sun.

Paris picks it up and chooses a goddess, I thought, staring pensively. *Cassandra says that will start a huge war among the mortals. But would that be preferable to a war across Olympus?*

I wasn't sure I could destroy the apple. Destruction was not my specialty. Therefore, *someone* had to keep the apple — and that someone shouldn't be me.

But I wasn't so sure the whims of Olympus should be allowed to cause millions of mortals' deaths — again.

Slowly, I picked up the apple. I stared at it.

Kallisti, it said. *For the fairest.*

I had been the only woman not affected. Even both my sisters had fought for it. The brawl had pushed the apple out over Olympus, down into the world of mortals. And I had known something must be done to stop Eris's gift causing further chaos.

A brilliant light exploded from the sky. Dazzling, the queen of the gods stood before me.

"The apple," she said, her voice echoing. "Give it to me."

I felt my eyes widen. The queen of the gods. Hera. I had spent my life avoiding her, afraid of what she might do to me.

Another light grew, this one up from the ground. It billowed into a rose and exploded into Aphrodite. She stood, radiantly, wearing absolutely nothing.

Hades, I thought numbly.

"*I* deserve the apple," Aphrodite sneered. "You must see I'm the fairest of Olympus."

"I am your queen!" Hera snarled.

Aphrodite smirked. "And men actually take an interest in me."

A third light stabbed the air and snapped into Athena. Clad in battle armor, she was wielding a spear.

Oh, HADES, I thought.

"Nothing is fairer than wisdom," Athena announced. "The apple belongs to me."

I felt myself sweating. All three goddesses had gone mad for the apple at the wedding. And a worse three, I could not have chosen. They were all infamous for their capriciousness and jealousy.

No wonder Cassandra predicted war would come of this. I felt sick. But I still had one hope: my mortal disguise was even better than Athena's.

"How could I choose?" I asked piteously. "You are all lovely beyond comprehension. I could never discern which is the fairest!"

Of course I was lying. It was clearly Aphrodite.

Aphrodite tossed her hair. Hera just stared at me stonily.

"I know!" Aphrodite cried. "Choose me, and you'll get the love of any man you wish!"

I tried not to show how revolted that idea made me. I knew what Aphrodite's idea of love meant. Cassandra had experienced that already.

Hera caught on quickly. "Give the apple to me," she commanded. "I'll give you power. Power over others, as well as your own destiny."

If I *had* been mortal and a slave, I would have gone for that instantly.

"Wisdom is greater than power," Athena said coldly. "Without wisdom, power and love will fade."

That gave me pause as well. But the real question was not whose gifts I wanted: it was whose anger would most likely be fatal to me.

Unfortunately, the answer seemed likely to be "all three."

"Will she who benefits protect me from the others' wrath?" I wheedled, making a show of cringing.

All three goddesses frowned. Athena looked suspicious, but nodded. Aphrodite sniffed and waved her hand. Hera folded her arms and glared.

"You'll find me very grateful," Aphrodite purred, holding out her hand.

"Nothing could protect you from my wrath," Hera growled.

"I defend those I like," Athena said coolly.

"All right." I swallowed. Here it was, then. "I give the apple to Aphrodite."

Aphrodite squealed and snatched the apple from my hands. "I knew it!"

Athena's eyes flashed. "The goddess of war is not the wisest person to offend."

"Nor the Queen of Olympus!"

"My reward, please!" I cried.

"Oh —" Aprodite looked up from the apple. "Of course. Certainly. Who shall I enchant?"

"Zeus," I said.

"*Zeus?*" Hera roared. "My *husband?*"

"To fall in love with Hera," I added.

There was a stunned silence.

"You want . . . Zeus . . ." Athena began slowly.

"To fall in love with *Hera?*" Aphrodite squeaked. "That's disgusting! I never enchant married people to fall for each other!"

"Please," I said, my palms sweating. "Please, Aphrodite. Half the problems on Olympus spring from Zeus's unfaithfulness. You could end it easily."

"Lose my greatest bargaining chip?" Aphrodite asked incredulously. "How would I make deals with mortals who want to have affairs with him?"

"Not to mention the power that would give Hera," Athena muttered.

"APHRODITE!" Hera roared. "You made an agreement! NOW FOLLOW THROUGH!"

"Fine," Aphrodite snarled. "I'll do it." She jabbed a finger in my direction. "But *you* get no protection from me."

Light exploded like sharp spikes, and she vanished.

I stood alone before Hera and Athena.

I swallowed, rubbing my sweaty palms on my tunic. *Please let them not recognize me. Please let them not recognize me . . .*

"You know," Athena said shrewdly, "one might say you benefited more than Aphrodite, Hera."

Hera's eyes went hard. She stared at me like she was tempted to blast me into ashes. "That mortal still chose *Aphrodite,*" she spat.

"Then I'll punish her," Athena said coolly. "I've received no benefit. And you know what I can do to mortals who offend me."

A slow smile spread across Hera's face. "Like Arachne . . . very well. I'll leave this mortal to be your plaything."

With a roar of thunder, she vanished.

Now I stood alone before Athena. Athena, who had turned a mortal into the first spider just for beating her in a weaving competition. Despite knowing the uselessness, my legs tensed to flee.

Athena surveyed me. Her face betrayed nothing.

"Which one?" she asked casually.

I gulped. "I — I don't know what you —"

"It never ceases to amaze me how imperceptive others can be," she murmured. "No mortal would make such a request. No mortal cares so much about wars on Olympus."

"They should. Wars on Olympus tend to affect all."

Her eyes narrowed. "And now you make me certain you are not what you seem. Who are you?"

"Aglaia," I admitted, raising my head. "Of the Graces."

"The goddess of *beauty?*" she asked incredulously.

"That's why the apple did not affect me," I said.

"Clever." She frowned at me. "I respect cleverness." Her frown deepened. "I suppose I'll spare you, as well."

She sliced the air with her spear, and stepped through the portal it created.

I closed my eyes, breathing raggedly. *I survived. Oh, thank Zeus, I survived.*

"Sister!" Thalia cried, dropping down beside me. "What did you think you were doing?"

"Fixing your mess," I retorted without opening my eyes. "Whose bright idea was it to invite every deity but Eris to a celebration?"

"Thetis just wanted the perfect wedding! You know what a dreadful guest she is."

Euphrosyne giggled, dropping down beside her. "Well, I think you did a good thing. Now we can go back to the festivities!"

I laughed. I hoped they were right.

But, after all, it isn't every day the Fates bow to Graces.

ADVANCED PRECOGNITION

"All right, class, get out your assignments. Yes, Miss Baker?"

Startled, Sarah raised her hand.

"*Yes*, Miss Baker?" the professor repeated, sounding impatient.

"Um," Sarah said nervously, "I thought this was our first day. What —?"

The professor let out a long, dramatic sigh. His eyes rolled heavenwards. "Every class I get a slacker. Of course I haven't announced the assignment yet; the *point* of this class is to remember things I haven't asked yet. As per our course aims?"

Sarah gulped, sliding down in her seat. "I — I don't think you've —"

"I hand them out on the last day of class." The professor gave her an irked glare. "Honestly, how —"

The whole class tittered.

"— did you even *pass* Beginning Precognition?" he finished.

Face burning, Sarah slid further down in her seat. She hadn't passed Beginning Precognition; she hadn't even taken it. She was here on a dare from her roommate, who had claimed that students on the Reason track couldn't possibly handle classes in the Mysticism building. Now she was beginning to wonder if her roommate had been right, and she'd been an idiot.

"No," the student next to her said.

Sarah stared at him, befuddled. What was he talking about?

"Miss Baker!" the professor barked. "Why aren't you taking notes?"

Sarah fumbled in her satchel for a notebook and pencil, and found her pencil had snapped in half. She turned to her neighbor. "Could I borrow —?"

"I already said no."

"Here." Someone held a pencil over her shoulder. "I brought this for you."

Sarah took it, relieved.

The professor put his feet up on the desk, pulled out a thick tome, and started to read. Sarah stared at him, stared at the blank paper in front of her, and looked around at everyone else. What were they all writing? How could they be taking notes when the teacher said nothing?

With less than five minutes of class-time left to go, the professor leapt up from his seat and talked at such a break-neck pace that Sarah barely managed to record five sentences. At last, humiliated, Sarah dropped the notebook into her satchel and buried her head in her hands.

I'm never, never, never going to pass this class.

"Don't worry about it!" the student behind behind her said cheerfully. "You've saved me enough times when I've forgotten things!"

Sarah turned around, startled. "Oh — uh — thank you for letting me borrow your . . . uh . . . pencil."

"Nice to meet you, Sarah! I'm Tanja. We're friends next week."

Sarah blinked. "Huh?"

"I have next period free, too!" Tanja looked delighted. "We spend it trying to figure out which paradox you have a mental block against. We figure out it's Salinski."

"Huh?" Sarah stared at her.

"Uh . . ." Tanja looked worried. "Did I forget to let you introduce yourself again?"

"Do you have trouble remembering the past?" Sarah asked weakly.

"Yeah," Tanja giggled. "I have an awful memory. The last time I tried taking a class in the Reason building . . . brrrrr." She shivered. "Can you believe the Logic professor claims looking at the answers on a test ahead of time is cheating?"

"You two might want to study together," the professor said from the front of the room, packing up his deck. "It's the only way either of you are going to pass."

"Do you think that's a threat or a future-seeing?" Sarah whispered, alarmed.

"Both," Tanja grinned. "'Foretelling your own actions and thereby making them happen.' That's Salinski!"

Tanja was a very, very confusing person to study with. If you could decipher her madcap insights and put them into some semblance of order, it was impressive how much knowledge she had. Unfortunately, she rarely remembered even half of what she knew.

"I hate this class," Tanja wailed, throwing her midterm in the trash. Both of them had failed it. Sarah was starting to get very, very worried about the final exam. "All the other classes I can just coast on through. Mind-reading? Easy. Clairvoyance? Please. I passed Supernatural Studies without even studying. But here, it's like the professor is trying to — to — to — *challenge* me!"

Sarah looked at her own test gloomily. She had only answered three questions correctly, and she wasn't even sure if that had been foreseeing or just guesswork. So far, she had only had two future visions she was sure were real, and both had involved Tanja complaining.

"And just *tell* Raine you're sorry," Tanja said, looking peeved. "It's getting ridiculous."

Sarah stopped. "What are you talking about?"

"The feud. It's so utterly stupid."

"Who's Raine?"

"It's not fair!" Tanja wailed. "If I'd lived two hundred years ago, people would have thought me brilliant! But now that we know paradoxes, seers can't sound mad anymore! We're supposed to make *sense!*"

"You could take medication," Sarah suggested. "I've heard time-drift potions can do wonders for —"

"And take a chance of losing all my precognition?" Tanja asked incredulously.

Sarah sighed. "Maybe we're doing this all wrong. You don't need help seeing the future; you need help remembering what you've seen. Have you tried using mnemonics?"

"Men-what?"

"People who can't see the future use them to study." Sarah looked at her test grimly. "People like me."

"I dunno." Tanja looked unenthusiastic. "If you mean memory tricks, those don't work on me."

"All right." Sarah held up a notebook. "Let's try something else instead. You have trouble keeping memory in your brain. So why not keep it on paper instead?"

Tanja stared at her. "On paper?" she repeated.

"Yes." Sarah tossed the notebook at her. Tanja fumbled to catch it a second early, and it fell to the ground. "Try writing whenever you remember something. Write in blue ink if you think it's the past, red if you think it's the future. I'll space it chronologically after the final exam. Then you can look at it during the final and see the whole class in logical order."

Tanja looked surprised. "That might actually work." She flipped the notebook open, grabbed a blue pen, and stopped. "It's blank!" she cried in horror. "All my hard work —"

"You haven't written anything in it yet."

"Oh. I could have *sworn* . . ." Tanja shook her head, dropped the blue pen in her pocket, and grabbed a red one instead. She plonked to the ground and started writing.

Sarah sat beside her and pulled out her home-made flash cards. She flipped the first one over and squeezed her fist in frustration. Eight times a day, she had reviewed these. She recognized the writing, the dents, the worn edges. But the terms had disappeared from her mind again. She *hated* those paradoxes.

"You're going about it all wrong, too," Tanja mumbled, not looking up from her notebook.

Startled, Sarah looked over at her.

"Studying. This isn't a class where you can learn things logically. You've got to use your intuition."

"What intuition?" Sarah muttered, glaring at the flash cards in her hands. "I don't *have* any intuition."

"Sure you do." Tanja snatched the flash cards and threw them over her shoulder. "Tell me about Jinkan."

Sarah squeezed her eyes shut, rubbing her fists into them. "Jinkan Paradox. Jinkan. Jinkaaaaaaaaaan . . ."

"Stop trying so hard. Paradoxes only work if you're not trying to remember them. What did you eat for breakfast this morning?"

"Huh?" Sarah gaped.

"Or tomorrow. Or yesterday. What did you eat?"

"E-eggs," Sarah stammered. "And toa— *Remembering the future at all when it is not predetermined!*"

"See?" Tanja said smugly. "Now tell me about Harighan."

"I don't —"

"For crying out loud," Tanja said in exasperation. "Just tell Raine to quit it and stop being stupid."

"'Changing what you remember from the future so that it does not occur'?"

"*See?* Now try Dinskan."

Sarah tried to let her mind wander. She stared at the walkway, the trees . . .

"'Confusing the future with the past'?" she asked slowly.

"No, that's Dinskan."

"You just asked me about Dinskan!"

"Really?" Tanja squinted at her.

"*You're* Dinskan."

Tanja grinned. "Kinagar."

"'Forgetting things you've prevented' — hey, this works!"

"Just try not to overuse it," Tanja cautioned. "Wringalin Paradox says the better you remember paradoxes, the more difficult it can become to think logically."

Sarah stared at her in horror.

"But I'm the living proof that's not true!" Tanja said happily.

In the end, Tanja passed their final exam with flying colors. Even Sarah, with the vaguest, fuzziest beginnings of future memory forming, scraped by. For some reason, that made the boy sitting beside her fly into a rage.

"She can't pass when I didn't!" he screamed. "It's not fair! She sat beside me to distract me! She *knows* I hate her! Of *course* I couldn't concentrate!"

Sarah turned and stared at him. "Who —?"

"You're such a jerk! I hate you!" He threw his test at her and stormed out of the room.

Sarah stared after him, jaw dropping as a fuzzy future memory tickled the back of her mind. "*Who* . . .?"

Tanja yawned. "Raine."

Sarah clutched her forehead. "There's someone just as crazy as you."

"Crazy, but with a passing grade!" Tanja crowed, waving her final test.

Beauty and Brave

Greyling was the first one to hatch. She smashed her way through the leathery exterior and lay flopping, gasping, in the mess of sodden, sticky slivers underneath her.

"Ugh. Grey scales," a voice noted from far above her. "You should call her Greyling."

Greyling lay sprawled with her eyes closed, panting and exhausted. She recognized her aunt's voice through a haze of exhaustion. Dragons spent three years inside their eggs, listening to the adults around them, so they hatched knowing how to speak.

Her eyes opened blearily, and she let out a gasp of shock. This was — it was — she knew no words to describe it. There were blurry images around her. What did this mean?

"Another egg is hatching!" Father's rough voice called.

Hatching. Slumped in her puddle of shards and goo, Greyling recognized the word. This was what they had spoken to her about for a long time. She let out a thin, wailing squeal of misery.

"Hush hush, Greyling," a comforting voice rumbled. Mother's voice. She opened her eyes blearily again. Mother's voice was coming from this huge . . . thing?

A shout from her father, and a chipping, cracking sound. One of the mounds beside her shattered. Something sparkling and glittering fell out.

"This one is beautiful," her aunt breathed. "You ought to call him Glimmer."

"Glimmer it is," her father said.

And that was the beginning of Greyling's childhood.

She felt a little left out with her other clutch-mates. Browning, Silver, and Brickie were typical size and colors, and could play with anyone they wanted fairly. Greyling was unusually large for her age, unusually heavy, and consequently rather clumsy.

"You'll grow into your size," Mother assured her. "You'll be glad you're so strong."

But all Greyling understood now was that she was too rough, too large, too clumsy to play with the other hatchlings safely. All she understood was that her size and her ugliness made her different in a bad way.

She wasn't alone in this, however. Glimmer, for all that he was beautiful, was too tiny and delicate to play with the other hatchlings safely either. They quickly became close friends, with Greyling as his protector. And when the other hatchlings played rough games that neither could be included in, the two of them went off to their hidden valley to play Capture and Chain.

"Did I tell you I saw a human here yesterday?" Glimmer asked, moving his hunter pieces across the mirrored surface. "Everyone says they're so small, but he was at least three times bigger than me. Capture."

"Chain," Greyling answered, moving her defender pieces forward to meet him. "Pierce or flee?"

"Pierce." Glimmer smirked. "Defend or retreat?"

Greyling eyed him. Her brother had a tendency to cheat. "Defend," she said slowly.

Glimmer paused to admire himself in the board's reflective surface — he was very vain. Greyling supposed she couldn't blame him for that, but it could get awfully annoying.

"Sword," he said, holding out a rough-hewn claw piece.

"Protect." Greyling scratched a loose scale off her underbelly, where they were the softest. She held it out to his claw piece. It stabbed through.

"Breach!" Glimmer crowed, swiping off one of her defense pieces.

"Hey!" Greyling cried, snatching his claw weapon. "This isn't one of yours! It's Father's! You cheated!"

"It isn't cheating when the rules don't say *specifically* you have to use your *own* loose claw bits," Glimmer said smugly.

"You know that's what the rules *mean.*"

"But they don't specifically *say* it! So it isn't cheating."

Greyling growled and moved her pieces.

"Capture," Glimmer said, his scales sparkling with excitement. "Piercing."

"Defense," Greyling snarled, scratching off a loose scale from her tail, where they were hardest. There was no way she was going to let him win this.

Glimmer ran the claw at her scale. The claw snapped.

"Awwww." Glimmer looked disappointed. "You really aren't supposed to use your tail scales. They're way too tough. It gives unfair advantage."

"You cheat, I cheat," Greyling shot back. "And do the rules specifically *say* it?"

"The rules for *you* should," Glimmer muttered, sulking.

"You know, you really should be careful around humans," Greyling said, jabbing his piece off the board with her claw. "Most hatchlings aren't as delicate as you are. I've heard humans like to capture crystal dragons as pets."

"Let 'em try," Glimmer said scornfully. "I can protect myself."

Greyling eyed him skeptically.

"Capture," Glimmer said, moving his hunters defiantly forward. "You gonna chain?"

When Greyling woke up in the morning, her brother was gone.

"Glimmer!" she called, alarmed. She was responsible for him, especially when their parents were gone. They had left the night before for their shift in the real-life defense chain. "Glimmer! This isn't funny! Where are you?"

There was nothing. She flew outside and searched the ground for his tracks. Sure enough, there they were: tiny claws, sharper and thinner than the rest of her clutch-mates'. She followed the tracks from the air, hoping he was just out gathering claw pieces from around the valley in order to cheat again.

Near the mouth of the valley, she reached the end of his tracks.

Since Glimmer couldn't fly yet, that seemed puzzling. Then she noticed something else that made her blood freeze.

Human tracks.

Her brother had been captured by humans.

Greyling let out a shriek of rage. She reared into the air and darted after the tracks as fast as her wings could carry her.

A normal dragon hatchling couldn't have flown as quickly as she did, or with as much stamina, but she didn't stop to think about that. She didn't pause to consider that perhaps the adults might be able to rescue him better. She needed to save Glimmer now, before worse things could happen to him.

Terrible images flew through her imagination. There were humans who killed dragons in order to use their scales and bones and claws as magic ingredients. There were humans who kept dragons to fight in horrible death match pits. There were humans who made dragons into trophies or killed just for the sport of it. Oh, how she hoped this human only wanted to sell Glimmer as some rich woman's pet.

She reached the end of the tracks more quickly than she had expected, and reared sharply. A campfire burned in the middle of a clearing, and Glimmer sat, mouth tied shut with cords, inside a wood cage. His eyes burned with defiance, and his wings drooped with misery.

Off to the side, the human was roasting meat. He was cursing in some human language, wrapping a bloody bandage around his leg. Greyling felt a surge of pride. Her brother had bitten him!

The human turned and saw her. He let out an exclamation. She dove straight for him and smacked her wing against his face. He fell over onto his rear, screamed in rage, and pulled out a sharp weapon.

Piercing!

Greyling swung her tail around, where the scales were hardest, and whacked it in the flat of the blade. The human screamed as it bent, held his arm, and then slashed it at her anyway.

Protect!

Greyling dove down to the cage which held her brother. She couldn't ram it — she didn't dare risk harming Glimmer — but she seized one of the wooden bars in her teeth and chomped through it.

Ow!

Her teeth aching, one of them bleeding, Greyling spun and thrashed the human with her tail just as he tried to slice her again. Then she bit through another bar.

Oww!

Glimmer's eyes brightened with mischief, and he rammed the side of the cage just as the human reared back at them. It budged just enough to trip him.

"Argghhhrrgggg!" the human screamed.

Wasting no time, Greyling seized another bar in her teeth and snapped through it. Glimmer, just barely tiny enough to fit through the hole, burst out beside her.

"Hurry!" Greyling cried, taking to the air.

The human came at them again, and Glimmer froze in terror. Greyling dove down in his face and smacked her wings at him. He thrashed and waved his weapon, trying to reach one of her wings.

"Hurry!" Greyling screamed. *"Run* already!"

Glimmer jumped and skittered as fast as he could out of the clearing. Greyling leapt back into the air, staggering as the human's weapon sliced through the tip of her wing.

She raced after Glimmer, pain stabbing through her sides with every wingbeat, the human crashing loudly after them. Then, just as she was about to collapse with exhaustion, she heard a roar of fury.

Father, an enormous steel-grey, rammed through the trees and smacked down on top of the human.

Greyling stumbled and fell to the dirt, feeling weak. She felt Glimmer creep up beside her and put his tail on top of hers.

"Going to get help was cheating," she mumbled.

She heard him laugh and cough weakly. "That's okay. It's not a game of Capture and Chain."

In the next few weeks, people started to treat them differently.

For one thing, Greyling was still weak and healing, so she caught a glimpse of what it felt like to be Glimmer: pampered and yet treated like she was too fragile to do anything. She found she didn't like it one bit, but she understood why Glimmer liked people fawning over him.

For another, everybody was impressed with their bravery, and Glimmer puffed himself up to take all the credit he could get away with. Greyling didn't mind; she was too weak to care about attention, and she knew he'd never been considered brave before, anyway.

When she was nearly healed, her aunt came by to visit.

Greyling greeted her cautiously, the last time she had seen her aunt having been at hatching. This was the dragon who had named her, who had called her ugly.

"Greyling," her aunt said, standing in the cave's mouthway.

Greyling nodded silently.

Her aunt moved forward. She hesitated, and then tore her claw through a bag around her foreleg. A glittering, clinking mass of gemstones spilled out.

Greyling gaped. *What in the world —?*

"I feel I owe you an apology," her aunt said stiffly. "I should not have cursed you with a hideous name. There is . . . there is an option that could give you beauty."

Moving forward, her aunt pushed several of the gemstones forward with her claws.

"Eat these," she said. "If you eat enough in early childhood, they can change your adult coloring. I was saving these for my own children, but . . ." She seemed to fight with herself, then pushed the rest of the mass forward. "But I think your need is greater. If you want beauty, you can have these."

Greyling stared at the pile of gemstones in astonishment. She'd never known there was an option other than being grey. A hint of envy fluttered in her heart. She could be admired, just like Glimmer. She could have her strength *and* beauty.

But . . .

"No." Greyling touched the pile of gemstones with her claw and pushed one back at her aunt. "I don't need them. Save these for your own children."

Her aunt looked shocked. "You don't —?"

"It's okay." Greyling curled her tail around herself. "Glimmer needs to be admired for something. I don't want to compete."

Her aunt looked troubled. "But . . ."

"It's all right." Greyling pushed the rest of the gemstones away. "I don't need to be a beauty. I'd much rather be brave."

The Dragon and the Santa

Irri's stomach growled as he flew. He hadn't eaten in three days, and he was extremely hungry. The elders had *warned* him against flying too close to the worldgate, but had he listened? Of course not, because he was the great Irri.

Irritably, Irri scanned the sky for birds. He'd seen precious few since he'd come here to this wasteland, and they had all escaped him. What kind of planet was this, all snow and ice? How could any reptilian person live in such a place?

A jingle made his ears prick up. In a distant cloudbank was the slightest red glow, dancing through it. He dove, roaring fire in his wake.

He seized his prey, a big woolly horned thing, and prepared to gulp it down.

"RELINQUISH RUDOLPH!" a voice roared.

Irri paused, looking down at the prey in his talons. It bucked and reared, showing the whites of its eyes. Defiantly, he moved it back to his jaws.

A blast of energy blew him back. With a shriek of terror, the woolly thing wriggled free. Eight more woolly things writhed from the cloud, and all nine stampeded away.

The cloud was silent for a moment. Then it said, "Blast."

Irri growled in frustration.

A round, red-and-white head popped through the cloudbank. From the lack of fear in its eyes, Irri surmised that this was not a prey species.

"Thank you very much!" the creature snapped. "Do you have any idea how long it takes to breed a reindeer with a glowing nose? Not to mention one that can fly! And they'll have scattered miles away! How am I supposed to deliver my presents *now?*"

"Need food," Irri growled. "Or I'll eat you."

"Dragons," the newcomer muttered. "Wait there."

The head disappeared for a moment. There was a rustling sound. Then a huge chunk of raw meat dropped from the cloud.

Irri shrieked in triumph. He seized it in his talons, tore his teeth into it, and gulped strip after strip of flesh. As the meat sizzled in his stomach, he began to feel a trifle better.

"You really shouldn't be in this world at all," the creature said, poking its head back up through the fog. "The last time I saw dragons was — oh — back when they still called me Odin."

"Came through by accident," Irri snarled, snarfing through his meat. "Flew too close to a gate. Turns out it was open. Closed behind me again."

"Ahh." The creature rubbed his eyes with two fat fists. "Of course. I could have told the humans that concentrating their world's magic on top of a pole, right around a solstice, was asking for trouble. But does anyone ever listen to me? Noooo. All they let me do these days is give their children presents. It almost makes me wish I was still Odin, even without the depth perception."

Irri bolted his last scrap of meat. He reared backwards, flapping his wings, and snuffed loudly for more. Sensing nothing, he narrowed his eyes in the direction of the escaped prey.

"Oh, no you don't!" the creature said from behind him. "You scared away my reindeer —*you're* going to pull my sleigh."

Sudden weight fell onto Irri's wings. He hissed and bucked in fury. But the creature behind him paid him no heed. More and more restraints fell around him, across his nose and face, until even his flame-centers were extinguished.

"Horrible creature," Irri gasped. "Release me!"

"No, I don't think so." There was a jingling behind him, and a string of little bells was heaved over his back. Irri bucked and shivered as the freezing metal itched him. The red-and-white creature paid this no heed. "I have few enough believers these days. I refuse to let you jeopardize the few I have left. Besides, there's nothing you can do about it. My magic's at its peak today."

Irri tried to spit fire, but nothing came. He writhed in fury.

"My current name is Sinterklaas, by the way," the round creature said, tying the last tether of its sleigh in place. "Or Weihnachtsmann. Or Santa Claus, if you insist."

"Hate you," Irri hissed.

"I'll send you home when we're finished. Unless you'd rather wait until the gate opens in another year?"

"*Hate* you!"

"If you must, but we've no time to waste on that silliness. Now . . . which one is closer from here, Greenland or Norway?"

Irri's opinion of the Santa did not improve as they continued on their journey.

The creature kept an enormous list that it flipped through incessantly. "Joseph . . . Emma . . . Johnny," it would murmur, making notes with either a thick feather or a black stick it called a pen. "I wish they'd let me upgrade to a smartphone, but not enough folks envision me that way."

"Why do you let them determine your life?" Irri growled. "It is stupid."

"Magic works best with the rules people believe in. I like magic. So I use the role they give me."

"It is stupid!"

"I've been worse," the Santa murmured, squinting at its long list. "Naughty . . . nice . . . I wish they'd give me a third option. Most children are both, and many things in between. Ah well, I never leave coal anyway."

Irri licked his teeth. Coal sounded tasty.

"There!" the Santa shouted, pointing at a cluster of lights. "Hold still while I freeze time so we can get down there safely."

The creature also had an irrational prejudice against hunting.

"No cats," the Santa told him firmly, as they hovered right over a rooftop with some tasty-looking fuzzballs on it. "No dogs, either. And if I catch you eating a horse, I will trap you until the next solstice comes, so help me."

Irri sulked as the round creature squeezed down a too-small chimney.

And then there was the food that the Santa *did* bring him.

"My reindeer are supposed to eat these," the creature said, dumping a pile of plants by Irri's mouth while they stopped to rest. "That means they're yours tonight."

Irri stared at the orange roots incredulously. "Do I look like a prey species?"

"Try eating like an omnivore for one night. It won't kill you."

Irri picked up the offending roots in his talons and flung them away.

The most annoying thing, however, was the way the creature kept *humming*. Sometimes it even added words, and the words were always inane.

"Up on the housetop reindeer pause . . . out jumps good old Santa Claus . . ."

"Do you *mind?*" Irri roared. "I'm trying to concentrate on flying!"

"Good for you. I'm trying to enjoy my one day out. I enjoy singing."

"You are tone-deaf," Irri growled.

"No, I'm not. Dragons just compose differently."

"You sound like half-dead rodents," Irri snarled.

"If you say so. But it's my sleigh. And there's nothing you can do to stop me. On the first day of Christmas, my true love gave to me . . ."

Irri wondered if the Santa was *officially* on a list of non-prey species.

✦ ✦

"That's it," the Santa said finally, pulling off Irri's restraints after a night that felt like it had lasted for weeks. "We've finished the last house. We're back at the pole. Ready to go home now?"

"Past ready," Irri growled. "Never want to see you again."

The Santa laughed. It sounded like a drum bouncing on a rock. "You know, you're the first six-limbed steed I've had since Sleipnir. It's been fun, hasn't it?"

"No," Irri retorted.

"You actually might stay," the Santa said shrewdly, unstrapping the harness. "Dragons are getting more popular every year. I'm sure you could cash in on quite a bit of magic."

"Not interested," Irri growled.

"In fact, given the hoardes humans believe dragons have, you could even do what I can't, and accumulate a lot of money." The Santa brightened. "Money that could fund Hollywood movies to shift public opinion about me . . ."

"Not listening!"

The creature put its arm around Irri's snoot. "We should talk about this further."

"You should *open the gate!*"

"One year. I'm sure you could stand that."

"I'm sure I could find a way to eat you."

The Santa paused. "Ah. Perhaps I shouldn't teach you magic to rival mine."

Irri showed off his teeth.

The Santa sighed and waved its hand. The portal opened.

Irri flapped his wings, rose in the air, and darted through it.

"Tell your friends the offer's open!" the Santa called as the portal sealed again. "Any dragon who wants to come next year could cut a great deal!"

Irri snorted fire in derision. He backwinged up into the red sky. As if he would send any of his friends into such a fate.

His *enemies*, however . . . now, that might be worth considering.

Invoice

To the United Nations:

We have received your payment for the oil received from planet Zybxx. It is insufficient. We asked for 850 human children, and you only included 809. Please make up this deficiency before we eat our dinner next week.

Yours cordially,
The Zybxx Corporation

Interplanetary Edition 

"Time is not a one-dimensional object," the pucker-faced old lecturer droned. "It has three that we know of. When the right frequency is hit by the disruptor . . ."

Kjino slumped against the walls of her cubbyhole, twisting her tail in circles. Her eggsister reeked of musty boredom.

"Why are they bothering to educate us?" an eggcousin beside them rumbled. He smelled acrid, like irritation. "It isn't like we're going to be experimenting."

Kjino's headcrest perked. Dull as the lectures were, she was excited for this journey. Imagine, traveling between the parallelities — to a universe where the *third* planet, not the ninth, had been the one to develop intelligence. The species developing this technology must be very clever. And they were going to put all sorts of people into a box and study them. She could hardly wait to be part of it.

"To be test subjects," Kjaila murmured, letting off the misty scent of yearning. "It's nearly as good as experimenting."

Kjino reached out her tail to clutch her eggsister's. She agreed. For a youngling, being tested upon was the greatest honor anyone could receive.

"I win again!" Aigiga crowed.

"I don't like this game," Jaya said stiffly, retrieving their spears. "The rules were not sufficiently clear. Only five hundred and sixty-eight —"

"Only three hundred are required for a casual game," Aigiga sniffed. "I understand the third-worlders believe in implied rather than stated rules, anyway."

Jaya ears tightened in fury. That rumor was false. It had to be. No civilized being would permit such vagarity.

"A rematch is permitted, if mutually desired. Rule seventy-three." Aigiga drew his spear across the blades of his belly, sharpening it.

Jaya calculated quickly. The status cost of losing would be lower than the cost of refusal. He had to keep his status high to stay qualified for the third-worlders' competition.

He rubbed his claws against itchy palms. The spears were built to irritate one's hands, to build challenge in the competition. "I wish to add sixty-three more rules before we proceed."

"I wish to add fifty-three myself."

Aigiga and Jaya stood, muscles locked to show strength, as they hashed out the rules of their rematch. With luck, they would be ready to begin in four days.

"Third-worlders look tasty," Gyorrrran told the others, drooling. "Fifth-worlders, too."

"Ninth-planeters hatch from eggs," Ygrrrrgyrn murmured, tongues dribbling over his teeth. "Egggggsssss."

The others rumbled as they feasted on the latest carcass they had trapped between them. The third-worlders lived on land, which meant the smorgasbord would be too much effort to trap and eat. But the promise of the feed still held such appeal that the hungriest had volunteered, anyway.

"Food from other universes," Rrrrgyrran rumbled, slashing his way through the half-fish that was his share of the trappings. "Taste different. New."

Gyorrrran's tongues snaked around and pulled out his favorite, rancid pieces. A social gathering meant feasting. He just hoped the third-worlders were tasty.

One master of the first world made a speech for his apprentice. "Honor."

Eeeoooiiii bowed low. "They wish for honor."

"Bestow," his master corrected.

Eeeoooiiii became grave. It was a terrible affront to misunderstand one's master. "They wish to bestow honor on all that they have chosen."

"Best."

Eeeoooiiii's spine liquefied, his mouth bitter with humiliation. To force one's master to speak more than once . . . and now *three* times . . .

Perhaps he truly did deserve the exile of attending the third-worlders' ceremony.

"I am sorry, master," he shouted, displaying his shame. Only those with valuable words were permitted to whisper.

The master turned and moved slowly back into a rock face. The air shivered as he vanished.

Eeeoooiiii meditated in case his master chose to emerge again. Then he prepared to leave for the third-worlders' ceremony.

"Get that banner up high!" one of the judges bellowed. "They'll be here soon!"

Assistants scrambled all around them, preparing for the aliens' needs. Off to one side were aquariums for seventh-worlders. To the front were breathing tubes for the first-worlders. Quartz sparkled on the banquet table for the second-worlders.

"I can't believe our research is being used for this," Elina, the biology consultant, muttered.

"It pays well," Darian shrugged. "Besides, the chance for me to practice sociology in front of a large audience . . ."

"The aliens are coming!" someone called, pointing out the window. "They're leaving the Center of Parallelities!"

"Get that banner up there!" the director screamed. "Get those cameras rolling!"

High above them, the banner unrolled . . .

Survivor: Interplanetary Edition!

"Ready?" the director shouted. "Set? And . . . action!"

<table>
<tr><td>SCHEDULE TMTR
(Form 1040)</td><td>Profit or Loss From Time-Travel</td></tr>
</table>

Part I: Income

1   Wages, salaries or tips . . . . ________
2   Gross receipts from predicting random events (including lottery) . . ________
3   Gross receipts or sales from disaster warnings . . . . ________
4   Income earned through stock market or interest . . . . ________
5   Income earned "inventing" future technology . . . . ________
6   Other income gained as the result of time travel . . . . ________
7   Add lines 1 through 6 . . . . ________

This is your gross time travel income.

Part II: Expenses

8   Cost of time machine, rental fee, or upkeep . . . . ________
9   Time traveler's checks and money exchange . . . . ________
10   Approved anti-anachronistic clothing for visits . . . . ________
11   Time traveler's insurance . . . . ________
12   Taxes, bribes and licenses . . . . ________
13   Add lines 8 through 12 . . . . ________
14   Subtract line 13 from line 7 . . . . ________

This is your net time travel income.

Part III: Exemptions

15   Qualifying ancestors (see instructions) . . . . ________
16   If you are your own grandparent or parent, count yourself twice . . ________
17   Sentient machines which require upkeep (see instructions) . . . . ________
18   Add lines 15 through 17 . . . . ________
19   Multiply line 18 by $11,332 . . . . ________
20   Subtract line 19 from line 14 . . . . ________

These are your total time travel exemptions.

Part IV: Fines

21 Persons informed of time travel in non-approved timelines . . . . _________
22 Paradoxes created and left . . . . _________
23 Cumulative severity of paradoxes (see instructions) . . . . _________
24 Multiply line 22 by line 23 . . . . _________
25 Historical events altered and not fixed . . . . _________
26 Cumulative severity of alterations (see instructions) . . . . _________
27 Multiply line 25 by line 26 . . . . _________
28 Add lines 21, 24, and 27 . . . . _________

These are your **total time travel fines.**

Part V: Credits

29 Tax paid paradoxically. Enter line 29 . . . . _________
30 Tax paid by possible descendents . . . . _________
31 Probability of those existing (see instructions) . . . . _________
32 Multiply line 30 by line 31 . . . . _________
33 Tax paid by certain descendents . . . . _________
34 Paradoxes averted (see instructions) . . . . _________
35 Cumulative severity of paradoxes averted (see instructions) . . . . . . _________
36 Multiply line 34 by line 35 . . . . _________
37 Add lines 29, 32, 33 and 36 . . . . _________

These are your **total time travel credits.**

Part VI: Tax

38 **Taxable income.** Enter line 20 . . . . _________
39 Tax (see instructions) . . . . _________
40 Subtract line 37 from line 39 . . . . _________
41 If not paid in future already, multiply line 28 by 125% (1.25) . . . . . _________
42 Add lines 40 and 41 . . . . _________

If amount on line 42 is negative, this is your **amount to be refunded.**

If amount on line 42 is positive, this is the **amount you owe.**

Sign Here

____

Dates

____

____

____

____

____

____

____

If more than eight dates, see instructions and check here . . . . _________

On the Way Through the Woods

"I say your charm thing is broken," Topaz yawned, dragging a brush through her unruly curls. "We've been walking for hours and haven't seen anything."

"The Forest Beyond is huge," Mildred said testily. This princess she'd run into was starting to drive her crazy. "Besides, I thought you weren't in a hurry."

"Oh, sure, sure." Topaz waved her hand lazily. "*You're* the one on an errand for your High Witch. I'm just off to teach my dad a lesson about frogs as suitors. Gingerbread?"

Mildred eyed the chunk of windowsill the princess had stolen from a house earlier. They had barely escaped from an angry, dessert-loving witch, and she wasn't eager to relive the experience. "No, thanks."

"Well, then," Topaz licked the last bit of sugar off her fingers, "want to make a detour? I see bushes off that way. They might have berries."

Mildred's stomach growled. "That might be okay . . ."

"Great!" Topaz hopped up and brushed the crumbs off her elaborate gown. She tugged her stockings straight, shook wrinkles out of her skirts, and marched towards the bushes. Mildred eyed the thick, dark trees in every direction and carefully brushed dirt off her black cloak.

"Hey, these aren't brambles!" Topaz called from ahead of her. "Come look at this!"

Mildred ducked under a branch and hurried over. Growing from the brambles were what appeared to be . . . "Flowers?"

"Not just flowers. *Roses.*" Topaz wrenched one off its stem and poked it behind her ear. "In the middle of a forest. Who would think?"

Mildred stared at the row of thornbushes, mind working with misgiving. They seemed much too tidy to have grown naturally —

A roar sounded ahead of them.

Mildred yelped, startled.

A figure in shredded clothing thundered through the brambles, shoving them aside in his wake. He looked like some monstrous cross between a human and dragon, with huge leathery wings and a fanged tail. His eyes glowed red with fury.

"YOU STOLE ONE OF MY ROSES!" the monster roared. "People who steal my roses must pay! People who —"

The monster stopped abruptly.

"*You stole one of my roses!*" he shrieked in an entirely different tone.

"You said that already," Topaz said helpfully.

"But you *actually* stole one of my roses!"

Topaz's eyes narrowed. "What, were you just going to accuse us either —"

"YOU WILL FOLLOW ME!" the monster roared, grabbing Topaz's arms with a clawed hand. "YOU WILL FOLLOW ME *NOW!*"

Without even seeming to notice Mildred, he wrenched Topaz's arm and dragged her off. In a moment, they had disappeared behind a thick clump of trees.

Mildred stood frozen, petrified. She was a witch. She was supposed to be powerful and terrifying. But she'd barely started school, and Menacing Spells was her worst subject. No matter what her teachers said, she didn't want to hurt anybody.

"You'll stay here till you've learned some MANNERS!" the monster roared.

"Really? That might take ages."

"*FEAR ME!*"

"No, thanks. Dad's got a much worse temper."

Mildred closed her eyes, breathed, and quelled the fear in her heart. She couldn't leave the princess alone with a monster, even if the princess seemed unworried. Slowly, she forced her quavering legs to move forward.

Past the brambles, beyond the thick clump of trees, she reached an enormous stone tower. Two massive rock doors were shoved open, and the monster stood in front of the opening, glowering.

Inside sat Topaz on a spiral staircase, fluffing her curls and making kissy faces at the mirror she kept in her satchel.

"H-hello," Mildred said hesitantly. "Are you — are you a human under a spell?"

"Who wants to know?" the chimera growled.

Mildred swallowed. "W-well . . . you have an accent from Guraton. I wondered . . ."

"Oh!" Topaz's eyes brightened. She tossed the mirror back in her satchel. "Are you from the royal family? Your face looks sorta like the old king's!"

The chimera glared at her. "That's none of your business."

"I heard a rumor one or two escaped the revolution," Topaz pondered. "You must've been cursed by the witch who helped it."

"None of your business!"

"A beast-curse," Mildred said, awed. "It must be. They're really tricky. In Traditions, we learned that the first was cast in the year —"

Topaz rolled her eyes. "Irrelevant, Mildred. How do we break it?"

Startled, Mildred shook herself. "Well . . . a kiss from a princess should work."

Topaz turned around and scrutinized the monster. "Yeah, not happening. Any other ideas?"

Mildred chewed on her lower lip. "One curse can supplant another — but it needs to be as powerful, and I'm not at that level yet —"

"Not a good idea to mess with curses. I've heard they can cause damage you don't predict."

"My Menacing Spells teacher said that doesn't matter."

"Your Menacing Spells teacher is a jerk."

Mildred fell silent. She didn't disagree.

"What part of 'none of your business' did you two not understand?" the monster rumbled.

"Wait a minute!" Topaz cried. "You know that spell someone used on my great-grandmother?"

Mildred scoured her memory. "You mean the standard rose-curse?"

"Exactly! Makes coma patients healthy, but puts anyone else in a coma. Don't you think this tower looks *awfully* like one of those?"

Mildred looked up. The enormous tower was covered in brambles, despite the fact that there were no cracks in the smooth stone to encourage this. The top window was covered in shutters with thorny vines growing into them. It had clearly not been opened in a decade.

"Is someone up there?" she asked softly.

The chimera snorted and folded his arms, turning away.

"Please," Mildred whispered. "We just want to help."

The wings flapped sharply and settled back onto his back.

"My sister," he said finally.

"Okay." Topaz hopped up. "I know what worked on my great-grandmother. Just a minute."

She skipped up the stairs. There was silence for a moment. Then an unearthly shriek.

"You *SLAPPED* me!" a woman's voice howled.

The monster gasped. He raced up the spiral staircase, tail crashing against the walls and smashing holes in his haste.

Topaz bounced down the stairs, looking pleased with herself.

"What did you do?" Mildred demanded. "What worked?"

"Same thing that worked on my great-grandmother." Topaz pulled an empty bottle from her satchel and shook it. "Revoltingly strong perfume. I keep one around in case I need to throw it at somebody."

Mildred stared at her. "The slap wasn't part of it?"

"That was for letting herself get cursed. I hate victims who play for sympathy."

"Rosa!" the monster howled from far above them.

"Beirran!" a woman's voice sobbed.

"And now his sister can kiss him," Topaz said with satisfaction. "Which is good, because I'm sure not gonna."

Mildred smiled. She set the directional charm again and pointed it towards their destination. "Should we give them their space?"

"Sure." Topaz hauled a rock candy cobblestone out of her satchel. "Want some?"

Mildred shuddered. "No, thanks."

They headed back into the woods. Mildred took one last look back at the stone tower as the view was covered by trees. She felt happier than she could ever remember being.

Witches aren't supposed to do good deeds, she thought, humming, *but the High Witch doesn't have to know about this, does she?*

"Besides," Topaz said casually, "I already stole the satin bedsheets."

When the Wilkinsons Grew

Strange things often happened at Number 42.

It didn't start out as the oddest morning. Mrs. Wilkinson was standing by the blue picket fence, weeding the bright purple roses that grew across the lawn like dandelions. Mr. Wilkinson's baseball game echoed across the street from their open downstairs window. In the side yard, Elsie and Alyssa were holding a tea party, Elsie dressed in frilly flounces and the baby covered in crumbs.

"Donovan!" my mother called from downstairs. "I want you to bring something to the Wilkinsons!"

I groaned, setting down my squirt bazooka. *Now?* Just when I'd set up a target? I reluctantly tossed my sister's teddy bear back into her bedroom and headed downstairs.

Bizarrely, Mom was standing in the kitchen. (My mom is the worst cook in the universe, so she usually never goes there.)

"Mr. Wilkinson was kind enough to bring us some produce from their tree," Mom said briskly, struggling to stretch plastic wrap over a paper plate. "I thought it would be nice to give them cookies."

"You're going to bake?" I asked skeptically. I looked at the plate. "Mom, nobody's going to believe those are homemade."

She yanked the plastic around the top.

"Mom, those are Oreos."

"It's the thought that counts," she said defensively.

I grabbed a plum off the fruit basket the Wilkinsons had given us. As usual, it was filled with crazy things. Kumquats, two peaches, five figs, a handful of seeded grabs, and some weird Chinese fruit called lychee. (I knew what it was because the Wilkinsons had given it to us before.)

"Why do they call that thing an apple tree, anyway?" I asked. "It grows everything *but* apples."

"They can call it what they like," Mom said. "Here." She dropped the plate in my arms.

I sighed, grumbling loudly for her benefit. But as I crossed the street, I grinned. What was Junior up to now? He wasn't in sight of either of his parents, which usually meant he was about to start something fun that was going to get us both in trouble.

Mrs. Wilkinson was grunting as she pulled at a particularly stubborn rose stem. She stopped, panting, when she saw me. Her eyes, normally the same brown as her skin, had turned light grey with effort. That was one of the odd things about the Wilkinson family: their eyes changed.

"Oh, hi, Donovan," she gasped, wiping her face. "I don't suppose you'd like to mow the lawn? I'll pay you . . ."

I made a face. I'd discovered that rose thorns could pierce through flip-flops. "No, thanks."

"Junior's watching a game with his father," Mrs. Wilkinson said, yanking at the rose, which uprooted extremely slowly. "You can join them if you'd like."

I peered through the window. Nope. No Junior. Yep. He was getting into trouble again.

Mrs. Wilkinson hurled the rose stem at a pile against the blue fence. Purple petals went flying everywhere. "There's a path I've weeded through there," she panted, pointing. "Would you bring Elsie and Alyssa a few blueberries, so they have something healthy to eat besides cookies?"

I rolled up the paper plate and shoved it in my pocket, hoping she wouldn't notice. "Sure. Did you grow any chestnuts yesterday?"

"Sorry," Mrs. Wilkinson said, wiping her brow. "The walnut tree's had cashews all week."

I plucked a handful of blueberries from the lower branches and looked for a good foothold to climb higher. Then I heard an almighty shriek.

"ALYSSA! ALYSSA! NO, DON'T GRAB THAT!"

I spun around and spied the baby, four feet tall and growing, pulling a lacy tablecloth off the doll table and starting to chew on it.

For a moment, I just gaped. This was new, even for the Wilkinsons.

"What in the world?!" Mrs. Wilkinson gasped. "Dear! Get out here!"

"Can it wait till the next commercial break?" Mr. Wilkinson called.

"*Daddy!*" Elsie shrieked. "Alyssa's *growing!*"

Mr. Wilkinson dropped his soda can. He ran for the screen door and flung it open. By the time he'd gotten outside, Alyssa was ten feet tall and pulling herself up on the house. *Thud. Thud. Thud. Whump.*

"My table!" Elsie wailed. "She kicked it!"

"Please don't scratch the paint, please don't scratch the paint . . ." Mrs. Wilkinson prayed.

Wham! Wham!

"Or break the shutters," Mr. Wilkinson flinched.

Jigglejigglejigglejiggle. The thirteen-month-old baby had discovered a storm drain. She giggled, shaking it, and water splattered all over us.

"I just don't understand," Mrs. Wilkinson said faintly. "What happened?"

"It's not my fault!" Elsie sobbed. "I didn't do it!"

"Of course it isn't," Mr. Wilkinson said darkly, his eyes turning black. "We all know whose fault it is."

As one, the Wilkinsons turned towards the house.

"*JUNIOR!*" they howled.

My best friend poked his head out of his bedroom window. He had painted his brown face with red and yellow war paint, and was wearing a feathered headdress. It looked ridiculous. "Yeah?" he asked.

"Would you mind explaining why your sister is now twenty feet tall?" Mrs. Wilkinson snarled.

Junior blinked and looked where she was pointing. "What the . . .?"

I licked the white stuff out of an Oreo, watching the baby rip the satellite dish off the top of the house. She waved it around with a fat brown arm and gurgled.

That's not going to do the baseball game any favors, I thought.

"You did this!" Elsie shouted. "Don't deny it!"

"I did not," Junior said indignantly. "Why would I want to grow the baby?"

Twenty-five feet tall now, Alyssa's pudgy brown fingers gripped the walnut tree. She ripped it out of the ground and gnawed on the top branches.

"Ohhhh, noooo . . ." Mrs. Wilkinson moaned, putting her head in her hands. "Dear, *do* something!"

Mr. Wilkinson gulped. "I haven't made an antidote for growth potion yet . . ."

"I have!" Junior cried, ducking back inside. "Just a sec!"

Thirty feet tall, the baby was shaking the tree, roots dangling and dirt flying everywhere, by the time Junior made it outside with a vial in his hands.

"Here," he panted, giving it to his father. "Make her drink that."

Mr. Wilkinson stared at the enormous baby. He looked back at the tiny vial. "And . . . how?" he asked.

Junior rolled his eyes. He marched over to the remains of the tea party, sorted through the broken cookies, and came up with one with chocolate sprinkles and a baby-sized bite mark in it. He popped the remainder in his mouth, chewing.

A moment later, he was shooting up twice as fast as Alyssa. He plucked the vial out of his father's hand and grabbed his little sister.

"Here, kiddo," he said, prying her mouth open. "Drink . . ."

Alyssa howled and wriggled, but he got a few drops in her mouth eventually. Then she started shrinking. Shrinking . . . shrinking . . . shrinking . . .

With relief, Mrs. Wilkinson grabbed the baby as she hit merely four feet tall. She shrank the rest of the way as she seized at her mom's hair, gurgling.

"See?" Junior called down in a booming voice.

We cringed and put our hands over our ears.

"Oh. Sorry." He sounded like thunder. "Just a minute . . ."

He tipped the tiny vial into his mouth and swallowed. He shuddered, and the house shook. Then he started shrinking. Down . . . down . . . down . . . down . . .

At last, Junior stood in front of us. The war paint was mussed, and he'd lost the feathered headdress, but he still looked ridiculous. He grinned, looking terribly pleased with himself. "See? No no, no need to thank me. Even though I just saved the . . . day . . ."

The rest of the family was glaring at him.

"How exactly," Mr. Wilkinson demanded, "did you know which cookie had growth potion in it?"

Junior licked his lips. "Er . . ."

"It was on *my plate*," Elsie added fiercely, jabbing his chest. "Alyssa just happened to grab it. You were trying to use that cookie on *me*, weren't you?"

"It was just a joke," Junior said sheepishly. "It would've been funny."

"*Funny?*" Mrs. Wilkinson snarled, pointing at the broken storm drain.

"*Funny?*" Mr. Wilkinson growled, pointing at the fallen nut tree.

Junior sighed. "I can fix the nut tree."

"Like you did for my rose bushes two years ago?" Mrs. Wilkinson asked incredulously.

"I'm so mad, I don't even want to *look* at you right now," Elsie snapped, her eyes crimson. "You keep away from me the rest of the day." She spun on her heel and marched back to the house.

Mr. and Mrs. Wilkinson exchanged looks.

"He *did* save Alyssa," Mr. Wilkinson said grudgingly.

"After causing the problem in the first place," Mrs. Wilkinson said in a clipped voice.

"But making the antidote first *did* show more foresight than usual," Mr. Wilkinson hedged.

Mrs. Wilkinson pursed her lips.

"We'll have to discuss what your punishment will be," Mr. Wilkinson sighed. "In the meantime, why don't you and Donovan go somewhere — far away from Elsie — and play?"

I recognized mercy when I saw it. We booked it out of there.

"Want to go bother *my* sister?" I asked hopefully as we ran across the street.

"Nah," Junior shrugged. "I have a better idea."

"What?" I asked.

He paused and dug two vials out of his pocket. There were still drops in them.

"So . . .?" I asked skeptically.

"So, you know how you've always wanted to ride a dinosaur?"

"Yeah . . ."

He shook the vials and grinned. "Would any giant lizard do?"

I looked at the glass vials. I looked at Junior.

"Awesome," I declared.

Author's Notes

Rite of Passage

My writing slowed to a trickle during college, research papers being the bane of my existence and very plentiful. Out of the few short stories written during those years, this was my favorite, and the one I rewrote most frequently.

When I decided to start publishing short stories on my website last year, I decided to start with this one because it felt representative of my style, and it was the strongest I had written most recently.

A Phone Conversation

Sometime during a summer vacation from high school, my siblings and I were sitting around the kitchen table eating lunch, throwing around sillier and sillier ideas. The best one of these turned into this very short short story.

A few years later, in late 2001, this was accepted in *The Leading Edge*, a local science fiction and fantasy magazine. When it was printed Issue 42, it became my second published short story.

The Spinning Talent

This was an idea I came up with in the middle of church one Sunday, during my first semester of college. Rather than taking notes, I scribbled an entire rough draft in my yellow notepad and then rewrote it later on my computer.

About six months later, I started developing *A Magical Roommate*, my comic strip that ran for eight years. The characters of Della and Aria heavily influenced my characterizations of Aylia and Alassa at the beginning of that story.

Unicess

I started trying to get published when I was fifteen. I wrote this short story my last semester of high school for a magazine called *Spellbound*, featuring children's fantasy, for an issue called "Wings."

It was ultimately rejected, but I found a home for it in a 2004 edition of *Beyond Centauri*. That made this my first short story written for publication, and my fourth that was printed.

Cindy's Fairy Godmother

My second short story written for publication, this was the first that was accepted! It appeared in the Winter 2001 edition of *Spellbound*, which had the theme "Genies and Other Wish Granters."

This short story bears a special place in my heart because it is the only publication I ever received while I was in high school.

Monster Under the Bed

My third short story written for publication, this was also my third accepted. It appeared in the Fall 2002 edition of *Spellbound*, themed "Things That Go Bump in the Night."

In my first month of college, I had the first computer I ever named: The Horror. It used to randomly crash and delete things, and if I didn't have backups, well, life would just stink. Shortly after this short story was accepted for publication, my digital file for it crashed-and-deleted. Receiving a hard copy of it a few months later was a huge relief.

Time Switch

When I started this in junior high school, it originally started out life as a book. Eventually, when I rewrote it in college, I realized that it didn't need to be any longer than it became.

I wanted to explore what happens when a person comes *back* from time-traveling, and has to deal with somebody else having lived their life while they were away.

The Apple of Discord

Taking a Myths, Legends, and Folklore class in college, it reminded me just how greatly certain aspects of Greek mythology irritated me. This short story shows some of the feminist in me.

I made sure to use only characters who are already in the mythology, and I put a great deal of research into this short story.

ADVANCED PRECOGNITION

While I was supposed to be taking notes the first day of class one day, my mind started wandering: "What if our teacher expected us to turn in an assignment on the first day?"

Naturally, this became another of my college-written short stories.

Beauty and Brave

I wrote this early this year for the Summer 2013 edition of *Spellbound*, "Dragons." They rejected it, but the poem I submitted, "One Midsummer's Night," did make it in.

I seem to like exploring the themes of beauty and the lack of beauty and what it means.

The Dragon and the Santa

This came up in much the same way as an earlier short story in this anthology: my siblings and I were laughing about silly ideas at lunch one day.

First written in high school, and rewritten in its final form recently.

Invoice

This originally came from a really long short story I wrote in high school that was drab and dull and preachy. Maybe ten years later, I realized that old dead thing would be really funny if I turned it into something super-short and pointed.

So I did.

Interplanetary Edition

Sometimes we humans have the oddest reasons for doing things. I felt like exploring how some alien cultures (from alternate universe versions of our solar system) might interpret science-project-that-needed-corporate-backing.

The original short story I based this on, written in junior high school, was called "Time Twists."

Schedule TMTR

Have you ever filled out a Form 1040? Tax forms are the most mind-numbingly boring things in existence. Naturally, I had to try making one to deal with the insanity of time-travel cliches.

I wouldn't mind having a few "possible descendants" paying my taxes for me.

On the Way Through the Woods

The short story I intended to write for the Fall 2013 edition of *Spellbound*, "Creatures of the Deep, Dark Woods," refused to gel completely. So, in a fit of last-minute frenzy, I decided to take the best deleted scene from *Black Magic Academy* and turn it into this short story. The reason I cut it from the book was that it seemed like a complete digression from the main plot, but I think this is the very reason it makes a nice standalone story.

It didn't end up in the issue, but the poem I submitted, "On a Long Camping Trip," did.

When the Wilkinsons Grew

I wrote this short story the most recently, so it seemed like the best way to finish off the anthology. I believe this makes the first short story where I have written in the first person from a male perspective successfully.

Intended for the Winter 2013 *Spellbound* "Giants" theme, I liked it so much that I didn't want to leave it unpublished when it was turned down, so I started this anthology.

About the Author

Emily Martha Sorensen lives in a noisy, noisy house with one-year-old twins, a three-year-old daughter, and a husband just as frazzled as she is.

She is the author and artist of *A Magical Roommate* (wizard-in-training gets forced to go to college in our world), *To Prevent World Peace* (a magical girl series . . . from the point of view of the villains), and the book *Black Magic Academy*.

To read more of her work, drop by http://www.emilymarthasorensen.com and see what's currently updating.

www.ingramcontent.com/pod-product-compliance
Lightning Source LLC
Chambersburg PA
CBHW022111050726
47591CB00002B/757